James Henry

Thalia Petasata Iterum

Or, a Foot Journey From Dresden to Venice, Described...

James Henry

Thalia Petasata Iterum
Or, a Foot Journey From Dresden to Venice, Described...

ISBN/EAN: 9783744797290

Printed in Europe, USA, Canada, Australia, Japan

Cover: Foto ©Andreas Hilbeck / pixelio.de

More available books at **www.hansebooks.com**

THALIA PETASATA

ITERUM,

OR

A FOOT JOURNEY

FROM

DRESDEN TO VENICE,

DESCRIBED ON THE WAY IN VERSE

BY

JAMES HENRY, M. D.

LEIPZIG,

GIESECKE & DEVRIENT, PRINTERS.

1877.

TO THALIA.

Put on thy hat again, sweet mountain maid,
And come and trip it as so oft before
Thou 'st tripped it with me over hill and valley,
Linked hand in hand, and not without the shell.
Come, and behind thee, for a season, leave
Thine own Aonian Mount and sisters dear,
And breathe with me new air, and see new sights,
And hear new sounds: there 's many a sight and sound
New even to thee in this fair world immense:
And trill with me a new song, not, I hope,
To be our last, and love me daily more,
As I will thee love daily more, for ever.
Come, come, sweet mountain maid, come once again.

ROSAMOND, Octob. 6. 1859.

"DRESDEN, farewell! we leave behind with pleasure
Thine eight long months of winter, lowering sky,
And clouds and smoke, a cutting north-east blast,
And bleak, bare land, without one hedge to shelter,
And trottoirs, upon which to walk secure .
Is, even for the adépt, a puzzling problem;
And rugged pavement, where each stone apart
Stands like a boulder, scorning all connexion,
All intimate acquaintance with its neighbours.
Thy grinding coal-carts, too, without regret
We leave behind to lumber-on incessant,
Awkward, unwieldy, ill-built, as it had been
The builder's aim to waste the drawing power,
And incommode the road, not draw the coal.
Nor even with feigned regret leave we behind,
To lord it undisputed óver both
The narrow, dusty highway's pathless sides,
Thine ever-trundling wheelbarrows and cradles,
And men and women yoked in the same traces
With dogs, and drawing the same common load.
Inhospitable, mercenary Dresden,
Thou that exactest from the weary traveler
A fee for the permission to remain
Even óne night in thy foul, ill-smelling city,
And following the example of thy kings,
Who reckon in how many years so many
Groschen per head for seeing will repay
The prime cost of a picture, driv 'st a peddling,

1

1

Mean trade in *aufenthalts-* and *meldungs-karten*,
And in *gebühr* tak 'st what the opener, bolder,
Honester robber takes by force of arm,
We turn our backs upon thee; there 's the fee,
For our *abmeldung;* count it, see it 's right,
And let us go in god's name, and the last
See of thy dogged, stiff-necked lutheranism,
Too rational for christian, and yet not
Rational enough and simple, not enough
From humbug and chicanery free, for pure,
Plain, unsophisticated atheism."

We said, and paid our ransom, and our faces
Turned joyful southward toward a kindlier soil,
And warmer sun, and people less severe,
Less strict, less puritan, more life-enjoying
And healthier. It is Tuesday, June the second,
Of the year eighteen hundred, fifty-seven,
The wind fresh from the north, Réaumur plus twelve,
Sunny and bright the sky, with white clouds spotted,
The Kreuzkirch' steeple chiming one, P. M.
Scared by our footsteps' sound as we pass by,
The old inhabitants of Strehla's pond
Cease croaking, and their skinny, wrinkled muzzles
Draw under water, and hide sedulous
From man, the universal enemy.
Under the linden shade we rest a while,
Sipping our beer, in Strehla's Restoration,
And looking back contented on the cloud
Of mingled dust and smoke, which all the long
Seven winter months we for an atmosphere
Palmed on our sore-recalcitrating lungs.

At Ober-Lockwitz turning to the right
Our way along a pleasant bottom leads,
Quiet and grassy green, and thick with trees
Of various leaf: maple, and graceful birch
With its white ribbony rind, and great horse-chestnuts
Poising on every bough's end their majestic

2

Pyramidal blossoms. Such the overwood,
With here and there a sturdy, strong-armed oak,
Protestant-like erect among his lither
More catholic neighbours. Birds of every song,
Blackbird and thrush and nightingale enliven
The hazel underwood. Apart sits dreaded
Upon his solitary bough the cuckoo
Bugling alone, and in the purpling rye
The quail-king crakes, and crakes, and crakes incessant.
Pale in the hedge euonymus, and bright
Spangled the grass with ornithogalum's star.
In the clean Restoration of the flour-mill
We rest again, and drink again our *töpfchen;*
Then onward in the evening's cool to Kreischa
And English Madam Thoman's *"rittergut"*
And the Bad-Anstalt, seeking in the latter
In vain for lodging; the Bad-Anstalt 's empty,
Desolate the rooms, the season not begun;
So forward, through the Lungwitz promenades
Rural, to Lungwitz, with the like success,
For in the Lungwitz *gasthaus* there 's a concert,
Music and dancing, all the beds engaged;
So on again, though tired, to Reinhardsgrimma,
Where we arrive at nightfall, sup on eggs
In butter fried, and each a pint of beer;
Then one hour chatting with the village doctor,
And reading riddles, weary go to bed,
And to a new day wake, refreshed, at six,
And wish each other joy we 're not in Dresden.

   The morning 's bright of Wednesday, June the third,
Réaumur outside at seven o'clock, plus seven;
Inside, plus twelve. At ten we 're on the road,
And quickly out of sight leave Veisner's inn,
And the last gable-ends of Reinhardsgrimma.
The Goldne Höhe down on us no more
Looks, on our right, no more the Wilischberg
— Both behind left towards Dresden — as we push,
Right in the sun's face, up the hill, toward Luchau

Under the wooded knoll, then down again
And up again and down, and up at last
To Johnsbach, where at twelve o clock we dine
On cold roast veal and bread and lettuce-salad.
"You 're surely not a German, Sir," I said
To a guest dining at a table near us
On *cervelàt-wurst* and one glass of brandy,
Soon followed by a second and a third.
"I 'm a Graubündner from the upper Rheinthal,"
Smiling said he, "and you 're an Englishman".
"Not badly guessed," said I, "though not quite right.
I 've not indeed the square Teutonic forehead,
Wide-sprawling mouth and solid chin and cheek,
And can affirm without yaw-yawing till
My own or hearer's stomach 's on the point
Of yielding-up its làst meal, yet I 'm not
Therefore an Englishman. A deep salt sea —
Alas! not broad enough — my little island
Divides from England. There in olden time,
Under their own laws, with their own religion,
Manners and customs and ancestral language,
Lived, harming no man, happily the Irish. '
But in an evil hour from England came
Armed ships across, and armed men leaped ashore,
Offering the hand of friendship and to teach
Better religion, manners, laws and language,
And by corruption part, and part by force,
— Woe to the weaker who lives near a stronger! —
Got, inch by inch, possession of the land,
Rooting the natives out, and in their place
Themselves establishing. I 'm of that stock,
In Ireland born, by blood an Englishman,
But not by sympathy." "As I a Swiss,
Politically, not by inclination,"
Said the Graubündner, drawing his chair toward us
In confidence. "There is no right but might,
And slow as is man's justice, heaven's is slower."
Our new acquaintance is a man of sixty,
Who of this great world scarcely less has seen

4

Than far-adventured Ithacus himself,
For he has been in Algiers, and has crossed
The Beresina with the first Napoleon,
A spurred and booted courier; nor since Fate
At Waterloo made short work of his master,
Has ceased through middle Europe's lands to carry,
Beneficent, the blessings of Denteia,
As, not unaptly, called by him the fay,
Whose care it is to mollify the pangs
Inflicted on humanity by Nature's
False, Nessus' present of two strings of pearl
Fair seeming, but in acrid venom dipped,
Pestiferous, malignant, the blood curdling,
Maddening the brain, embittering the sweet life.
So after dinner we set out together
Comrades well matched, the doctor and the dentist
From Johnsbach downward into Müglitzthal
At Bärenhecken; thence along the Müglitz
Upwards toward Bärenstein's baronial castle,
High on the solid gneiss rock on the right.
We seat ourselves upon the mossy bank
Provided on the roadside for the traveler
By Kammerherr von Lüttichau, and drink
Out of the fountain opposite the jet d'eau,
And wander in our minds back to our lodgings
Four years ago in Dresden, in the street
Built by, and surnamed after, Lüttichau;
Then onward to the tin-mill, see the crushing
And washing of the gravel to obtain
The shining metal, more than silver useful,
And scarcely less resplendent, and look back
On Castle Bärenstein behind us left,
Over the valley and dark beech wood towering,
And, humbler, on the saddle of the hill,
Stadt Bärenstein, in name alone a city.
The Müglitz next we leave, and up the hill
To Lauenstein upon the left ascending
And Lauenstein's once strong, now mouldering *schloss*,
Make early halt, drink coffee, sup and sleep

Im Gasthof zur Stadt Teplitz, greeted there
By the smiles unexpected of an old
Dresden acquaintance, the Silesian housemaid
Of the *Trompeter Schlösschen*, housemaid now
In Lauenstein, *im Gasthof zur Stadt Teplitz.*

Brilliant as yesterday on Reinhardsgrimma
Rises to-day on Lauenstein the sun,
Though Réaumur here, high in the Erzgebirge,
Shows three degrees less heat. At seven we 're forth,
Inhaling glad the buoyant upland air,
And by our yesterday's companion still
Escorted courteous. Rested on the frontier,
And drunk our first Bohemian beer, and plucked
Some golden Geum sprigs and Alchemilla,
We stand at noon upon the Mückenthurm,
Commanding wide the prospect of the valley
And town of Teplitz — granges, corn fields, spires,
With grassy knolls in fair confusion mixed,
And naked rocks and dark pine-woods Hercynian,
By Spitzberg peak shut-in, upon the south,
And Milleschauer, loftiest of the blue
Mittelgebirge. In the midst, the Schlossberg
— Acropolis abrupt — its huge boss rears,
Crowned with the ruins of Dobrowska Hora,
And looks down upon Teplitz and the valley.
Here the Graubündner, at his tether's length
Arrived, parts from us, to return alone
To Bärenstein; we from him part not glad,
For he has seen the world, and more of men
Learned from themselves than we from all our books.
Down from the Mückenthurm our way to Teplitz
Leads on direct through Graupen, on the left
Leaving the Wallfahrtsort Mariaschein,
Not the first Wallfahrtsort which we 've passed by
Irreverent, on our pilgrimages various
To art's or nature's lovelier, holier shrine.
Built by Loyola's calculating sons,
More than one hundred years ago and fifty,

6

An old investment now 's Mariaschein,
Yet pays its dividends punctual, and its shares
Rise in the market, and the Virgin's credit,
Shaken a while, stands firm to-day as ever.
Im Gasthaus zum Tiroler-Hof in Teplitz
Arrived at three we meet our Dresden friends,
Lutheran Pastor Haase and his wife,
And Moritz Léndemann, the accurate,
Faithful translator of my Adversaria,
To Teplitz come to spend the Whitsuntide,
As in old times the English came to Bath,
The Roman conquerors of the world to Baiae,
For Teplitz is the Czechish Bath and Baiae,
And Bath and Baiae signifies in Czechish.
"No, if you set a value on your life,
Or personal comfort, you must not through Böhmen,"
Said with a warning voice our honest host
Of the Tiroler-Hof, a Dresdener
And Lutheran. "No you must nót through Böhmen,"
Said Pastor Haase, "they 'll maltreat and rob you,
Murder perhaps; they 're catholics every one,
As bigoted as the Devil and as wicked."
But we were Irish, and not unaccustomed
To hear the English protestant so speak
Of Ireland and his catholic Irish brother,
And turned a deaf ear, and through Böhmen forward!

Teplitz behind us left, and Teplitz' bathers
And roguecries and follies and ennui,
And the last protestant faces, we set out
On Friday, June the fifth, at ten o'clock,
Along the dusty, carriage-traveled road,
Soon for a lane exchanged, where more at ease
We wander, plucking wild thyme, and admiring
The full rich purple bloom of the Anchusa,
And red of the Adonis, here first time
Presented to us in the name of Venus,
Wet with the Goddess' tears or with the dew,
It's all alike now, even the Goddess self

— Mother of love and beauty, foster-mother
Of the Acncadae — has gone the way
Calcanda semel hominibusque deisque.
And listening to the cuckoo in the wood
On either hand, or to the lark above us
Filling the blue sky with his minstrelsy.
At one we dine in Dux, at three drink coffee
In Brüx, where the first kukuritz salutes
The southward-wending traveler's longing eye;
The other crops are northern; vetches, beans,
Oats and potatoes, rye and wheat and barley.
The road 's on either side with apple trees
And pear trees garnished, as in Würtemberg,
But a week's journey brings you to no vine.
Henbane luxuriates, and a delicate Lotus,
Unseen by us before, adorns the road
With its pale sulphur, almost primrose, bloom.
We pass between the Spitzberg on the left
And Schiessberg on the right hand, and arriving
Towards eight at Welmsschloss, in the lower inn
Meet — nay, not murderers, but civility
And kindness and good supper and good bed.

Saturday morning's splendid, June the sixth;
And we enjoy it, early on the road
After an early breakfast, while the lark
Is still upon his first flight, nor has yet
Dipped from the golden clouds to greet his mate
On her eggs sitting in the clover field.
High on its hill above the Eger see
The walled-in town of Saatz. A promenade
Of sweet robinia in full blossom leads
Steep from the chain-bridge upward to the portal
Narrow and Gothic-arched, and by a tower,
Which for defence might once have served, surmounted.
The chain-bridge reached ere noon, and climbed the *Anlage*,
And a last backward glance of admiration
Cast from above upon the variegated
Wide landscape spread below, and bridge, and Eger

Rushing to meet the Elbe at Leutmeritz,
And cleared the portal, guarded now no more
Unless by the toll-gatherer of Saatz,
We cross the "Ring" enlivened by the Fair,
And in "zum schwarzen Bären" rest and dine,
And hear Bohemian music. An Iopas,
Blind and in tatters, sings how fair the world,
Of love and beauty sings, and on his harp
Plays, to amuse, while his own heart is breaking.
Onward, at half-past twelve, through Reitschowitz
And Milschowitz, and up the bare, bleak hill.
Under a solitary elm, mid-way,
Sleeps, on the grass, a full-accoutred soldier;
His helmet, laid beside him, and his sword's
Bright polished scabbard glitter in the sunbeams.
My daughter, less gallant than sleeping Milton's
Inamorata, earns no pair of gloves,
Leaves in the sleeper's hand no penciled sonnet,
But turns away indifferent and explores
The many-tunneled dwelling of the wasp
In the soft sandstone of the roadside rock,
And curious marks how the sagacious builder
Has every separate tunnel's opening lengthened
With a projecting, downward-curving porch
Of sandstone particles agglutinated,
So as to exclude at once both wind and rain,
And keep the interior homestead dry and warm,
And queries with herself: if so indeed
Sagacious were the builder, and not merely
Bent to get rid of inconvenient rubbish.
Sceptical query! met by answer prompt:
Doubly sagacious, to so manifest
Purpose to turn mere inconvenient rubbish.
Of Albion's shore the chalky soil reminds us
As we draw near to Flöhau, where at six
We drink our coffee, and had gladly slept,
Tired and with eight miles to the next night-quarters,
But in the house are carpenters and masons,
And our host, with a rudeness little Czechish,

Gives us to understand we 're not quite welcome.
So on the inhospitable "Hospoda"
Turning our backs ill-pleased, we follow-on
Through Strojetitz, the rugged, half-made road.
The taper poles stand stately in the hopyards;
The dresser, stooping, guides with gentle hand,
And to their bases binds the curling shoot
With double straw halms; or, his day's toil ended,
Draws on his coat and, weary, plods toward home.
Poterium Sanguisorba, purple Lychnis,
Tall, virulent henbane with its jaundiced blossom,
And gray leaves spreading like a prince's plume,
Daisies closed for the night, campanulas,
And silvery potentillas the road garnish
On both sides with a variegated limbus.
The cuckoo ceases not; the evening thrush
Answers the cuckoo; and the bat whirrs by.
Below us on the right, off side the valley,
The solstice sun — candescent all day long
In cloudless empyrean, and, arrived
At his day's goal, candescent still and sparkling —
Turns into chrysolite hill, road and valley,
And on the left-hand chrysolite projects
Our silhouettes gigantic grown since noon.
Cooler the air; we don our coats, and quicken
Our steps though tired, and, as the full moon rises
Ruddy behind the pear-trees, reach, ere yet
Quite sunk the day, our "Grün Baum" inn in Jechnitz.

The landlord 's a rich, comfortable boor
Who shows us small politeness, and next day,
Sunday, the seventh of June, at half past eight,
We leave without regret our "Grün Baum" inn,
And on through Dlesko village and the village
Of Poderzanka, living sight or sound
Observed in neither, and, ascending slow,
Arrive ere noon, and dine at Hoch Libén,
High on the bare, bleak hill's comb. Onward then
Through the *meierhof*, where, as we rest a while,

Tired, on the green sward, overhead a falcon
Comes, on his black and white sails hovering noiseless,
And round about us wheels in airy orbs,
Alighting oft, and oft upon the wing —
Challenge to ús to spread our pinions out
And spurn the ground, and cleave with him the air.
In vain! the fetters of our destiny
Confine us, and away he soars at last,
Leaving us there to clank our leaden chain.
Lonely the country round, and lonelier still
The red-pine forest, by no sight or sound
Of living thing enlivened, yet not dismal,
For, overhead, between the pine-tree tops
We see in patches of still-varying form
The glowing sapphire of the summer sky,
And underfoot tread less the partially
Sun-mottled shadow of the dark pine wood,
Than the reflexion of the vertical sun,
Variously by the táll pines intercepted.
Arrived at Plass ere three, and by a large,
Full glass refreshed, each, of black, milkless coffee,
We pay our visit to the convent building,
Convent no more, since by the godless hand
Of Kaiser Josef, in the year of grace,
One thousand and seven hundred five and eighty,
Dissolved the holy brotherhood Cistertian,
And carried-off to Prague the plate and jewels.
A less ungodly Josef, Josef Streer,
Plass' *pfarrer* and *decàn*, receives us kindly,
And through the building courteously conducts,
And tells us how seven hundred years ago
King Wladislaus, tired all day with hunting,
Here in the wild wood spread his mantle out,
And laid him down to sleep, and, in a dream,
Saw coming toward him wide-mouthed a she bear
With her two cubs a-gallop, and awaking
Sudden, affrighted, scarce sufficient timely,
Blew on his horn and called his huntsmen round him,
Ere on him wide mouthed came the bear a-gallop

With her two cubs, which while the huntsmen thwart
With spear and hound, and harry through the wood,
The good king down again upon his mantle
Laid him to sleep, and dreamed he saw in Franken
Stately with tower and cupola, a cloister
Cistertian, tapers in the chapel lit,
The brethren singing vespers in the choir,
And, waking, vowed a vow with tower to build
And cupola, upon the site, a cloister,
Match of his vision's, and to call it Plasst,
Because 'twas on a mantle, *plasst* in Czechish,
He dreamed the dream which warned him of the bears.
"Behold him there, king Wladislaus second,"
Proceeded the *decàn,* and to a picture
With his forefinger pointing, read the scroll:
"Vivat perpetuas in aeternitates
Hujus cœnobii fundator pius."
And there beside him see the second founder,
'Titel — der zweite Trojer' — who rebuilt,
Only one hundred years ago and forty,
Stately as here you see, the ancient convent
Grown grey with time, and mouldering, and there 's Tängler,
The pious abbot, who some years before
Rebuilt the church. And see this sacristy;
How lofty, noble, plain and unaffected!
In similar style a néw church, and to form
One building with the sacristy, was projected,
When the strong hand of power dispersed the brethren,
And to profane use turned the cloister building:
Here's the post-office; the gendarmerie
Have here their quarters; there's the village school-house;
Part 's empty, and part 's let to individuals;
The parish priest, your servant, Josef Streer,
Has here apartments; the refectory
Lodges the superintendent of the district;
And in the once right noble *Prelatur*
— See standing there apart the massive pile —
Fürst Richard Metternich, *patronus Plassii,*
Rusticates threé weeks, every second summer.

So having said, and shown us the whole building,
And on our way accompanied a while,
Asking us many questions about Ireland,
And Ireland's only hero, only man,
Daniel O'Connell! — ah, gone to his audit —
The courteous Pfarrer to protecting heaven
Commends us, and takes leave, and toward Plass turns
His slow, age-stricken step. We bid farewell
Grateful, and up the hill alert to Ribnitz,
Less than an hour by the old road direct,
And, safe arrived with sundown, sup and sleep.

The morning sun of Monday, June the eighth,
In vain shines for the sluggards, who sleep on,
As if till seven there were no day in Ribnitz.
Scarcely at half past eight we 're on the road,
Scarcely at half past nine the dark wood enter
Of red-trunked Scottish pine, near Kasenau.
Grateful to dazzled eyes and sweating skin
The expanded green umbrella of the wood;
Grateful the cool grass of the long allées
To the hot, dusty feet; but water's none:
Few springs or brooks in this high lying land,
And even the few that were, by ten long days
Of drought have been dried-up — stay, what means this?
A full-length statue of Saint Nepomuk
Here in the middle of the wild, wild wood!
Lo! the starred nimbus radiant round his head,
And cradled in his arms the crucifix:
There must be water near; Saint Nepomuk
Signifies water; in his single person
Embodies the whole company of Naiads
And river-gods, for modern superstitions
Are comprehensive, and one modern idol
Answers the purpose of a thousand ancient.
We take a narrow pathway to the right
Behind the statue, come to a draw-well,
Bucket and ladle, and, our thirst assuaged,
Return and pay our compliments to the saint.

In Tremoschnà at one o'clock we dine,
Content, not being Jews, upon pork cutlet,
But without coffee after, for our hostess
Will not, or cannot but of chicory
Make coffee; so we leave the bitter draught
For knaves to sell and easy folk to swallow,
And parliaments to label: "chicory";
And onward through the Scotch fir-wood toward Pilsen,
Under a darkening sky and gathering storm,
And distant thunder growling in the east.
Scarcely before the rain, arrived at three
We cross the Mies bridge, and the market-place
Crowded with pilgrims to the Heiligenberg:
Women and men, each one with staff in hand,
And stockings soled with felt, and white hemp wallet
Over one shoulder slant across the back.
Way-worn they all seem, whether in groups standing
And with each other taking serious counsel,
Or under the shop windows seated supping
Their barley porridge, and their black bread slicing,
Or sleeping stretched-out at full length beside
The church-steps in the middle of the Platz,
A spectacle to move the heart to pity,
Less for the pilgrims than unhappy man
Full of his hopes and fears and to no purpose
Jack-o'-the-lanterned through a quagmire world.
We spend in Waldeck's excellent hotel
The rainy evening, writing home long letters,
Reading newspaper garbage, drinking coffee
— The fragrant Arab bean, unchicoried —
And early sup and early go to bed,
And early wake — alas! to a rainy day.

I never liked a wedding — the rejoicings,
For me, have always less of joy than sadness, —
But of all weddings saddest is to me
Pluvious Jove's wedding with prolific Terra.
Dreary to me the thick, damp, misty air;
The leaden, lowering clouds; the sun's eclipse;

Nor ever without horror do I hear,
Th' artillery salvoes or the startling flash
See, of the fireworks; nay, there's not for me
In all the empty realms of sound, a sound
Duller or more monotonous than the patter
Of the black nutshells upon roof and windows.
Our letters posted, and the sky become,
Toward noon, less uniformly thick and murky,
We dine compendious, and along the smooth —
And dry, despite the rain — quartz-sanded road
Set out alert for Przestitz, flowering lindens
On either hand and sycamores in seed,
And white robinias scenting all the air.
Rádinaberg uplifts, upon our left,
Its dark pine woods and Waldstein's crowning castle;
Over green waving fields of wheat and rye
Our eye expatiates wide upon the right
To Weipernitz's whitewashed church and gables.
'Cross the Radbúsa then, and up the hill
Along the poplar-colonnaded street
Of Littiz' smiling, scarce Bohemian, village;
For here we leave behind the Sclavish race
Of stock Bohemians, and begin to meet
German Bohemians and the German language,
To us, accustomed almost from our cradles
To Schiller's countrymen and Schiller's tongue,
More than the Czechish grateful to the ear,
More than the Czech congenial to the heart.
Adieu at Littiz to the sycamore,
Linden and sweet robinia promenade,
Damsons receive us now, with poplars mixed,
A stunted row on either side the road.
It rains and clears and rains again and clears
Ere we reach Schlowitz and a glass of beer,
Two hard-boiled eggs each, and a half-hour's rest.
Suspended by two cords between two posts,
Edge upwards, hangs before each house in Schlowitz
A four-foot long and two-foot deep hard board,
And, by the finger pushed or by the wind,

Swings freely to and fro. A string hangs over
The board's edge, and on either side descending
Suspends two hammers, each of hardest wood: —
"What means this swinging board, these swinging hammers?"
Said I to a hussar who on a bench
Lay wrapt-up in his long white riding-cloak,
Half lounging, half asleep: — "That board 's the *Klopfbret*"
He answered civilly, "and with those hammers
Three times each day, as regular as the sun,
At morning, noon, and evening foddering hour,
We rattle on it, to call out the boors
To bring our horses corn and hay and water."
The Magyar hussars behind us left
To batten upon Schlowitz, we pursue
Along the pear-and-damson-garnished road,
Under a leaden, sometimes showery, sky,
Through an ungenial land, our evening way,
And ere three hours see rising right before us,
High on the hill, the massy church of Przestitz,
With its unfinished steeples — better so,
Than to completion brought the ugliness.
Przestitz at five reached, we put up our horses, —
That is, our tired selves — at the Austrian Kaiser,
Przestitz 's not too good, though best, hotel,
And, after coffee and an early supper,
Gladly to béd go and sleep sound all night,
And wake next morning to more rain, more rain.

"The thirsty plants and arid fields admire
And bless god's providence for this fine wet morning,"
Said to me on the stairs a pietist,
Meeting me coming down from my bedchamber, —
For in half barbarous Przestitz as untiring
As in enlightened London, pietism
Ceases not to obtrude, on learned alike
And on unlearned, its oft-convicted lie: —
"Nay," replied I, with so much piety
Of voice and manner as on só short notice,
Not being an adept, I could well put-on —

16

"Limit not so the providence of god;
Not your parched uplands only, but the hay
That lodged lies rotting in the valley bottoms
Praises god's providence for this fine wet morning;
The swagged and drooping wheat-halm, of its pollen
Washed by the heavy raindrops, and left barren,
Praises god's providence for this fine wet morning;
Even the poor widow, who, two hours ago,
Lost in the river's flood her only son,
Praises god's providence for this fine wet morning;
And I, for my part, every morning rising,
Make it a point to bless god's providence
For the good weather he has pleased to send,
And only when my thanksgiving is ended,
Out of the window look, to see what weather,
Wet, dry, or cold, or hot to send has pleased him."
Dinner at twelve, at half past two black coffee
— So called and paid-for, but of chicory made —
And, the sky brightening, we set out at last,
Réaumur at plus thirteen, the rain still dropping,
And up the southward road before the wind
Go drifting half, half rowing. Schwihau Stadt
At half-past five affords us bread and beer
And not unwelcome rest. The evening sun
The clouds had scattered and, resplendent shining
Down from the pine-clad hill's comb on the right,
Threw Schwihau castle's shadow on the river,
And flooded holms, and steeped in golden light
The road before us and the left-hand hills.
Conspicuous with his starry coronet,
The patron Saint protects the double bridge
Under whose arches the swollen Oglava
Makes her way north, toward Pilsen and the Mies.
Tall aspens tremble either side the road,
White flocks of geese the léa graze, white Spiraea
And flowering clover perfume all the air.
After two hours of various hill and valley,
Woodside and rivulet and sheep-browsed knoll,
And marshy hollow full of meadow saffron

Maturing only now its last year's seed,
First at Stiepanowitz we come in sight
Of Klattau on the rising ground below us
Dim through the twilight peering with its tall
Pointed black tower and white two steepled church.
One half hour more, and in the great gaststube
Of Sandner's White Rose inn upon the Platz
— Within the shadow of the tall black tower
And white, two-steepled church together jammed
Into the left hand corner of the Platz --
We 're snug at supper seated, veal discussing,
Salad and stewed prunes and Bohemian beer,
And our most patient lungs to a mixture treating
One part tabacco smoke and two parts air.
At ten the Zimmermädchen with black silk
Bavarian kerchief bound about her head
Concealing hair and forehead and both temples
And hanging down in two long queues behind,
To our room leads us, bids us "*Wohl zu schlafen*",
And shuts the door, and we sore tired to bed
After we 've first with scarce requited trouble
Our ingenuity racked to make commodious
With help of tablecloth and sofa cushions,
Our incommodious, dumpy, German cribs.
Grumbler against heaven's ways I blame thee not,
In other items whatsoe'er thy fortune,
If thou hast often in a German crib
Passed a long, weary, restless, tossing night,
Praying in vain for day and leave to stretch
To their full length once more, thy crippled limbs.

  Next morning, Thursday, Corpus Christi day,
Comes to our door, the kellnerin knock knock,
And, though I 'm in my shirt, must be admitted
Instanter, being on pious business bent
All things, even decency itself, must yield
To pious purpose: populus dat sacris,
Dat pater ipse viam. "In God's name"
Writ on the Cesar's crown secures it more

18

Than all his legions. So my chamber door
Opened without delayt, I make my bow
And look respectful on, while from the window
The kellnerin in honor of the day
Hangs out a garland of green walnut leaves
And full-blown tulips, peonies and roses.
And on a peal of churchbells and a clang
Of trumpets from each corner of the Platz
See, slow and solemn out of the church door
Evolves itself the Frohnleichnam's procession!
Helmets on head and steel blades at their side,
The men of war come first, in double file,
About two hundred. Judge them by their looks,
Not one of them could find it in his heart
To harm a mouse; they are Christians every one,
Disciples of the meek and lowly Jesus,
Who broke not the bruised reed, the smoking flax
Who quenched not, but his life upon the cross
For them gave, freely, and for us and all.
So are they, by their looks judged, and thou 'rt not
Fool enough, reader, by their swords to judge them,
Helmets, cartouches, and last year's compaign.
Next comes a gorgeous banner, gold and crimson,
Flouting the wind; a lamb its meek device.
A choir of boys next, and, in spotless white,
Their hair with roses wreathed, a choir of girls,
Singing the Lamb and of their office proud,
Gay looking round with unaffected air.
With heads uncovered bearing each in hand
A lighted taper, the lay brothers follow
Of charity so called, and the lay sisters.
Then the Frohnleichnam's banner high upheld
By eight strong arms and by two cords before
And two behind, kept steady and from swaying,
Displays the mystery that sets at nought
Touch sight and taste and smell and understanding.
Under a canopy of cloth of gold
See, next, the bishop, splendid in ranchmantel,
The monstranz in his hands. One page before him

Carries his mitre, one his pastoral staff,
Two pages bear his train up, clouds of incense,
From silver censers flung, precede and follow.
Which is the God? Which is it has the worship,
He or the bit of kneaded flour and water
He carries in the monstranz? Every knee
Bows as he passes, every head is bared.
To kiss his garment's hem, to touch the cross
Broidered in gold on his white satin shoe
Is a foretaste of heaven. That man 's a fool
Who dreams of shorter path to power and honor
Than through the temple of the people's God.
Caesar was high priest ere he was dictator.

    At half past nine set out, at half past one,
— Little of new observed upon the way,
Except Parnassia spangling white the marsh,
And plots of flowering poppies the bauer's heart
Gladdening with promise of the racy oil,
And further on, upon the left, the church
And dorf and meierhof of Bieschin,
And further on still, on the right, the real
Wide branching antlers of the painted stag
Upon the Wirthshaus' wall of Hořakow [1] —
Dine in the rural inn zum Grünen Baum
In Czachrau village, high on the steep hill.
We sit in th' inner Stube, the host's bedroom,
Amidst old chests of drawers and brown oak tables
And three-legged stools, and hard, wood-bottomed chairs.
A crucifix in one corner on the wall,
Up near the ceiling; in the opposite corner,
A churn-dash and a churn half full of milk;
A trestle in the middle. On the trestle
A keg of beer whence ever and anon
The landlord's son, a tall, gaunt youth of twenty,
In long blue stockings, short black leather breeches,
And shirt-sleeves, draws for the guests in the outer stube,

---

[1] Pronounced Horschakof ř being pronounced like rsch.

And scores the full pot, never not remembering
To take first sip of each, lest 't should be poison,
Or overflow unseemly on the board.
Commend me to the youth, I see him still
Bending his knee joint, canny, and his tall head
Under the lintel ducking, as he slips,
Beer-pot in either hand, out of the inner
Into the outer stube, one step down,
The Ganymede of Czachrau on the hill-top.
At half past two, again upon the road,
Pushing our upward way to Gesseny,
Vaccinium nigrum,[1] and her fairer sister,
Vitis Idaea, and the tinkling cowbell
Tell us, at last, we are entering the mountains.
Nor is it long till our and their sworn friend
And old acquaintance, Arnica Montana,
With her rich triple bloom, repeats the news,
Confirmed anon, if witness more were needed,
By modest, lowly, blue Pinguicula
And every midge trapped in her viscid leaf:
We leave the dusty, long, circuitous road
And take with joy across the elastic lea
The shorter, steeper, upland path to Brunst,
Where, the lea left, we plunge into the thick,
Desolate, neglected, hoary Böhmerwald,
Following a path at first, on whose green edge,
With wood Anemone and Campanula spangled,
We pluck, then first time to our eyes presented,
A Paris quadrifolia, aptly named
From Ida's handsome youth. But soon the path
Fails, and we miss our way and wander lost
In the wild wood, tall trunks on every side
Standing erect, of aboriginal pine,
In family groups, son, father and grand-father,
Or prostrate rotting where the trenchant axe
Of age, unpitying woodman, felled and left them.
Gray they are all with lichen, and with mosses

---

[1] Vac. myrtillus called by the Romans Vac. nigrum. See Fea (in Lemaire's Virg.).

Variously bearded; nor above our heads
Hangs not Usnea down from every bough
Her long, lank, grizzled hair. Far to the left,
Among the pine trunks moving, something white
Fixes at last our anxious, searching eyes,
As distant lighthouse in the deep, dark night
The wave-tossed mariner's. It 's a bawsint cow
Led by a man and boy, who by good fortune
Being bound for Ascherle, not much aside
From our direction, guide us through the wood's
Entanglement and set us on the road
In full view of the Arberberg, and scarce
From Eisenstein an hour, last town Bohemian
And our night quarters, where at eight arriving
And putting up at Fuchs's White-Rose inn
We sup in a Gaststube thronged with boors
Carousing, and the Corpus Christi day,
Early awaked with penitence and prayer,
Putting to bed with song and dance and glee.
The Jäger most they sang who with his dog
"Behutsam geht den finstern wald hinein";
Sweet the guitar chimes in and, side by side
Goes with the jäger and his faithful dog
Into the *"finstern wald hinein"* the fiddle.
In at the door and open windows peep,
Half bold, half shy, delighted listening faces
Of boys and girls. A bullfinch on the wall
Above the music strains his little throat,
Or in the intervals a solo sings
Delicious. We almost forgive the morning
And leave them happy, and go tired to bed.

The clear, cool morning, Friday, twelfth of June,
Sees us from Eisenstein at nine o'clock
Down toward the frontier pushing — but what 's this?
A board shaped like the bottom of a coffin,
Against a roadside elm leaned, with the scroll:
The dead-board this of Wilhelmina Gerstner,
Who in the lord died happy, July fourth

Of the year eighteen-hundred-two-and-fifty:
Her years were eighteen. Pray for her, good christians.
And here about this aged linden's trunk,
See, sloping stand three, four, five, six, such boards,
Memorials all of souls which, passed away,
Would fain by the surviving be remembered,
Memorials all of corpses on them laid
Warm from the deathbed to be bathed with tears
And for the last time kissed ere laid apart
In the grim, darkling, dismal, silent tomb,
With their forgotten forefathers to moulder.
Therefore I praise the dead-board in the gangway
And trodden path placed, greeting the wayfarer.
And to surviving friends, too dainty nice
To endure the neighbourhood of mouldering bones,
At least recalling the orthography
Of a once loved friend's name. Fain, too, my name
Elsewhere I'd have inscribed than on an urn
In mausoleum or forsaken vault.
Here in this book behold it, therefore, written
And thrown in the frequented ways of men,
To catch the eye of passing friend or stranger
And gently force, from thought at least, a visit
To the lone inmate of the unseen tomb.

And now behind us left in Ferdinands-thal
The Czechish frontier, and Bavaria entered,
A broad smooth road with grass on both sides bordered,
Friendly invites and through the red-pine wood
Faithful conducts us. It 's the forester's house
That peeps so pleasant out into the sunlight.
Above the door the stag's horns; round about,
The lettuce garden, gay with bachelor's-button.
A little further on we recognise
By his fusee across his shoulders slung,
And suit of gray, green hat and pheasant's feather,
The forester through the green wood coming toward us.
A rustic follows carrying on his shoulder,
Shot with a ball right through the velvet muzzle,

A yet warm roebuck — Ah, poor, harmless beast,
From Nature's tyranny, safe at last, and Man's!
Coffee and hard-boiled eggs in Ludwigs-thal,
At half past twelve, and visit, after coffee,
To the glass factory of polite Hans Streber.
We see the natron, see the pounded quartz,
The melting of the metal and the blowing,
The splitting of the cylinder, and heating,
Gradual, and flattening, and with a long-handled
Heavy, hot iron smoothing out so plane,
That, laid flat on a perfect marble level,
It bears uninjured a weight superimposed
On every square foot of a quarter hundred.
Washed with quicksilver next we see the foil,
And on the washed foil laid the crystal plate,
And pressed each square foot with a quarter hundred.
Oozes at every edge the superabundant
Quicksilver, and, the amalgam close adhering,
Behold to thine astonished eye presented,
In a transparent atmosphere etherial,
A second self, a second earth and sky,
Sun, moon and stars and living, moving world.
Adjournment to the garden then and greenhouse,
And coffee, and a half-hour's conversation
And not unwelcome rest in great arm-chairs
Amidst half cared exotics, for our host
Some years alone lives widowed and the orphaned
Garden and greenhouse miss the ever careful,
Kind and beneficent maternal hand.
Mutual farewells at six, and down one source
Of Regen purling in his stony bed,
We follow-on our evening way to Zwiesel
Where Kammermeier's inn zum Deutschen Rhein
With friendly courtesy receives us tired,
With supper entertains, and puts to bed.

Next morning after breakfast, tracing back
Some twenty minutes our last evening's way
Against the nórth wind, Reaumur at plus seven,

We pay a visit to Theresienthal's
Hollow-glass factory, see the melting, blowing,
And staining of the metal ruby red
With golden oxide, or with cobalt, blue,
Or white with arsenic; see the moulding, shaping,
Cutting, engraving, polishing and gilding,
And, with all forms and colors, painting true.
Herr Ernest Zimmerman, the company's factor,
Politely shows the processes, and explains,
And fain had sent us to Elisienthal,
To see the great glass-founding factory
And the gigantic offspring of the mould,
But neither on our way Elisienthal,
Nor we in the art of casting huge glass mirrors
So curious as the Nürnberg Company's factor;
Therefore direct to Zwiesel back and dinner,
And on, at two, from Zwiesel up the Aschberg
Shady with tall birch, rough with granite rock
Out-cropping gray upon the rich soft carpet
Of mingled moss and bilberry and whortle;
Then cleared the hill's comb and behind us left
Zwiesel, and Regen valley, and the Arber
Four thousand feet, and more, above the sea,
Down by the sloping, sunny, southern side,
To Rinchnach in the green and meadowy bottom,
Not without some short minutes pause to admire
The three-armed spruce gigantic which o'ershadows,
Midway, the slope, and with the emblems hung
Of Man's guilt and Heaven's justice, and the pact
Between the two irreconcilables,
Beguiles the kneeling rustic's weak, fond heart.
On then, from Rinchnach, through the meadowy bottom,
Taking off shoes and stockings where the brook
Has by a foot o'ertopped the stepping stones,
And through the opposite hamlet on the hill
And past the grim glass-factory and between
Green fields of rye and cross the virgin lea,
And through the pine wood, up hill now, now down,
To well named Kirchberg's church upon the steep,

Prospect-commanding hill, and our night quarters
In Hirtreiter's beer-brewery *am Hof.*
Our landlady's a pattern — not of beauty,
On Germany of all lands seldomest
Smiles Alma Venus — but of portly size,
And growth exuberant in all dimensions.
Her eye composed, apparel rather rich
Than ornamental, and air dignified,
Declare the house's mistress and the Juno
Of Herr Hirtreiter and high Kirchberg hill.
Not long we parley ere to the best chamber
The Kellnerin conducts us, serves with beer,
And bye and bye with supper; daylight fades,
And ere first candle lit, we 're safe in bed,
And on high Kirchberg not unsoundly sleep.

Sunday fourteenth of June, the bell has rung
For prayers in Kirchberg church, and young and old,
Women and men, their way uphill are wending,
As we descend, to gain by the new road
The rising lea before us, Reaumur showing
Scarcely thirteen, the wind chill at our back,
The low sky drifting with us. Soon we have left
Kirchberg behind us, opposite side the valley,
And as high stand or higher. Vast the wood
Clothing on either side the watershed,
And lone as vast. Only the cuckoo's note   ⟍
Breaks the dead silence, nor by other leaf
Than birch or beech the pines' monotony varied.
At last, far side the comb, below us opens
Over the forest's skirt a spreading vista
Of undulating plain and hill and valley,
Dotted with villages, and by the broad,
Stately, meandering Danube intersected.
By Paddling and Rohrstetten we descend,
And by the sculptured granite stone[1] which tells

---

[1] The inscription is engraved in a granite tablet which is in relievo but has
no cross. Fluting round bottom of tablet where it is set into pedestal.

Where fell, by treacherous shot out of the thicket,
— Fifteenth September 'twill be five full years —
Sebastian Hilz, th' aged landlord of the inn
At Euschertsfurth: pray for his soul, good Christians!
Perpetual winds the road, now on the verge
Of marshy meadow, on the knoll's side now,
Here in the poplars' shadow, open there
Between broad, fenceless fields of hemp or teazel
Or blue kohlrabi, or late millet braird
Tender emerging from the cotyledon,
Till Auerbach's little inn receives us tired
And shelters friendly from a thunder-shower
Which on our steps the last two miles has hung
Darkening the cheerful sky, and, with a lunch,
Timely recruits, of eggs and bread and beer.
Onward again at four the gallant sun
At last victorious, in full flight the clouds,
And spangled joyful every bush and flower
And millet ridge and teazel top with diamonds
Across the Oh, at six to Hengersberg,
And down the left bank of the sluggish stream
To Winzer, at the Burg's foot of that name,
Where we take up night quarters at the krämer's
Inn unpretentious, sup, and soundly sleep.

Our landlord's son next morning up the Burg
Escorts and shows us the wide prospect round
Of the great Danube basin: Nesselbach
To the south-eastward and Hofkirchen spire,
This side the river, opposite, Kenzingen;
South-west the Damenstift of Osterhofen,
Memorial of the battle on that site
Won by the Christian, by the Avar lost,
On Easter-day one thousand years ago;
Northwest, away upon the extreme horizon,
The hill and church of Bogen, longed for goal
Of many a way-worn, slow Bavarian pilgrim;
Nearer, the separate hill of Natternberg,
Offside the river, marks the embouchure

Of Isar, here not rolling rapidly;
Nearer us still, northwest, this side the river,
Hengersberg and its two hills and two churches
And the once famous Niederaltaich cloister,
Southward green slopes surmounted by the Hardt's
Long, black, unbroken line shut in the view;
The northward roving eye rests on the Daxstein,
Tripartite Rusel, and the Bichlstein's
Commanding summit, where on Benno day,
Every revolving summer, Baier meets Baier,
And eats his wurst, and drinks his pot of beer,
And looks down, happy, from his canvas tent,
On happy Baiern. In the middle rolls,
Swollen by the recent rains and fresh accrued
Regen and Isar, at our feet, the Danube,
And, flushed and overweening, floods the holms.
The heaped up ruins of the draw bridge piers
Afford us passage 'cross the grass-grown moat,
And on the walls we stand of Winzer castle,
The walls that once were, now mere heaps of stones
Disjointed, and with clematis wrapped round,
Kind plant that fain the ravages would hide
Of cruel Time and far more cruel Pandours.
Agriot and pear mark still the garden's site
And flowering elder blooms where once the rose.
Descended and till next day putting off
Our onward journey, we retrace our steps
Upward along the Oh's deep, silent stream,
Gathering sweet-william and tall yellow goat's-beard,
And white spiraea odoriferous,
And sallow comfrey with the purple lip,
And the sanguineous cornel's blossom white,
And orobanche not too proud to prey
On Thymian's humble root, and vicia cracca,
And yellow Iris bordering the water,
And stately virgin's-bower, and meadow-rue.
With such a nosegay we arrive toward noon
At Hengersberg, and after rest and coffee
In Westermeiers, towards two at Niederaltaich's

Cloister once famous and on Danube's right,
On Danube's left now, and no longer famous,
Time having with one potent hand dug out
A new bed for the river, with the other
Dispersed the Benedictines, and converted
To purposes profane the convent buildings.
Only the house, so called, of God remains.
A hundred years have fled and six-and-twenty
Since Joscio, seventy-third in the long line
Of Niederaltaich's abbots, celebrated
The thousandth anniversary of the cloister,
Performing high mass in the present church,
His own foundation, and then four years finished;
Read the inscription in the sacristy,
And how he brought from Rome and here enshrined,
Each in his crystal chest, the holy martyrs
Julius and Antoninus and great Magnus,
Noble Aurelia and most patient Julia
Behold apparelled all in cloth of gold
Crimson and clinquant, on white satin couchant,
False carbuncles for eyes, and, in the holes
Where once the breath of life played to and fro,
False sparkling emerald and sardonyx.
Upon their chapped, cracked, brainless skulls gilt crowns,
Withered palm branches crumbling into dust
Beside, not in, their well-knit once and taper,
Now dislocate and separated, digits —
Behold, if thou hast courage to behold,
The grisly skeletons, and, sistered with them
Couchant in like glasscase, on like white satin,
Her belt suspended from her fleshless wrist,
Widowed Alruna, Cham's most holy countess.
Thou hast beheld? Well, leave them there to shock
The living sense and curdle the heart's blood,
And come with me and visit in the convent's
Once potent priory the parish deacon,
Johann Aumayer, and the parish deacon's
Worthy assistant, Peter Anzenberger,
And having paid thy compliments and taken

A glance at parting at the full-length portraits
Opposite the windows in the sitting-room
— This here 's Mauritius, the church's patron,
That there in the rauchmantel is Saint Gotthardt —
Return with us along the Oh-to Winzer
And in the honest kramer's inn sup cheap,
And soundly sleep and wake betimes next morning
To keep us company down the Danube's side.

Who that had seen th' unclouded sun, last evening,
Setting in glory, had foretold, ere morning,
A frost, to flowering cereal and fruit-tree
Far and wide fatal? who had tearless seen
The unclouded sun this morning glorious rising
On field and furrow thick with icicles?
But we nor glorious sun unclouded rising
See, nor disastrous hoarfrost, but in bed,
Falsely luxurious (we can not deny it,
Elegant minstrel of the fourfold year)
Lying till seven, and breakfasting at eight,
And scarcely on the road at half past nine,
Pursue through Mitterndorf our onward journey.
In Sattling on a roadside tablet greets us
The pictured legend of Saint Isidore,
The ploughman's patron: lo! he leaves his plough
Still-standing in the field and goes to church
When the bell rings for vespers, and, returning,
Finds a winged angel down from heaven descended
Guiding his plough and oxen, and more land
Ploughed in his absence of one short half-hour
Than, had he by the plough staid, he had ploughed
Himself in a whole day from morn till night.
Therefore the poor Castilian ploughman's now
Blessed Saint Isidorus, plough and ploughman
Have now their patron, and the fifteenth May
Is Isidorus' feast through Christendom.
Our course is with the Danube. On our right,
Onward it rolls, the deep, majestic stream,
O'erflowing, here and there, the meadowy holms,

And, with its yellow wave, the alders bathing.

To

Professor Hutton
University College
Toronto
Canada

With the Compliments of
Dr James Henry, Trustees

from

Emily Malone
Stormanstown House
Glasnevin
Co Dublin
Ireland

Over the inclosure gate nailed *in terrorem*
Hawk, kite, and buzzard and, despite his caution,
Sly reynard caught at last. Through Söldenau
At half past five and on through Kam we pass,
And in the protestant town of Ortenburg
Stop for the night and sup in the inn zum hirsch,
Well named, for never finer pair af antlers
Adorned gast-stube wall. At seven next morning
Reaumur stands in our chamber at plus twelve.
We breakfast and set out, behind us leaving
Ortenburg's separate standing, vine-clad houses,
Each with its sweet robinia at the door,
And, high above them towering on the hill,
Ortenburg Castle, and at the hill's base
Eastward and south from Ortenburg and forming
With Ortenburg one protestant cummunion
— A little sturdy, rocky isle of truth,
Believe itself, in a vast sea of error —
Dorf Steinerkirchen and tall steepled church,
And take our way by Afham mill south west
Under the splendid-shining, not hot sun.
With pear and cherry, hornbeam, oak and linden
Variously furnished our ascending road
And still ascending, past Einöde Fuchshub
And past Salvator's convent secularized
And past Salvator village Steinhardt Wood
Then rises steep before us thick and dark
With various foliage and to test severe
Putting our lungs and gastronomic muscles.
But now and then from some commanding knoll
Or ridge's comb, our anxious, longing eyes
Refreshing with short glimpses of the still
Far distant Noric Alps: — "Stay! that's the Watzmann,
And that's the Dachstein; that, the Hohe Goell,
And look along this vista by the axe
Cleared as of purpose in the forest's thickest,
Yon level line's the summit of the bleak
Tannengebirge." Easy the descent
And reached in forty minutes from the comb

32

The chapel on the Kronberg over Griesbach.
Stone seats invite us and we rest a while
Under the lindens' shade beside the portal.
On one hand the Calvarienberg and kirchhof
Fair on the other the long range of Alps,
Blue tents of giants halted on their march
Or in entrenched camp whiling the long winter.
Then down the linden colonnade to Griesbach
And lunch of wine and coffee at the Post
Passing by Ostermünchner's better inn
And brewery, unknown to us till later,
And paying for our ignorance no less
In hard cash than in stoical endurance
Of bad fare, worse attendance and some rudeness.
Warned by the chiming clock and westering sun,
We 're on the road again at half past two,
And, frail memorial of our passing visit,
A full-blown garden rose plucked from the hedge,
Griesbach behind us leave and down the hill
Through the pine wood trip lightfoot, cross at Schwaim
The dull, canal-like Rodt, and, climbed ere five
The heights of Assbach (Ah! the convent church
Belongs now to the parish, and beer 's brewed
Where once the Benedictine brothers nestled),
At six reach Roththalmünster, and put up
In Wochinger's hotel, and sup and sleep.

Next morning 's little Corpus Christi day,
And all 's astir betimes in Rothalmünster,
Bells ringing, muskets firing, not one wink
Of sleep from five o'clock for weary traveller.
At seven, the platz swarms full of crowds expectant,
In holiday attire, men, women, children:
Banners stand at the corners. From the windows
Hang scarlet draperies, ribbons, garlands green.
At eight the bell tolls out and from the church
Winds solemn forth and stately the procession
What like if thou wouldst know, its picture 's painted
Above at Klattau, only the priest here

(It being little, not great, Corpus Christi,
And Rotthalmünster but a market town,
Officiates for the bishop, and in place
Of Klattau's full two hundred men at arms
Walk peaceful here the four men of the fire-watch.
At nine behold us once more on the road
And from the pine-clad hill's brow looking down
Upon the Inn before us, broad and bright,
Seaming the vale as with white satin ribbon,
Upon its long course from the Engadine
To Passau and the Danube. We descend,
And forward! up the valley toward the river;
And Malching passed and Malching's green-roofed church,
With wine refresh us and beef soup at Ering.
Splendid the day and happy smiles the valley
On both sides of the Inn's broad silvery band.
Haymakers in the fields. Their ruddy cheeks
By broad white stráw hats shaded from the sun.
Blithely they sing as in long files they turn
And toss the grass out to the glowing ray.
Beyond the river on the left our view,
South-east and south, expatiates to the Alps,
Here white with snow, there cloud-capped, baring there,
Their furrowed foreheads to the imminent orb.
Low hills with walnut green or swart with pine,
Close on our right hand, bound toward north and west
The wide spread basin on whose edge our road
Fringed with sweet-william and silene nutans
And yellow latyrus and medicago
And salvia, white and purple, and anthyllis,
Winds pleasant with us toward the Austrian frontier
And bridge at Braunau cross the deep, broad Inn.
I love the Inn, and never without pleasure
Look down upon its waves of beryl pale green,
Whether, at Silva Plana, from the foot
Of snowy Julier issuing meek and mild;
Or in loud cataract at Finstermünz
And Landek roaring; or its broad bright flood
Rolling majestic round the walls of Kufstein

And under Braunau's long extended bridge;
Or where it pours into the dark brown Danube
The contrast of its purer, clearer stream.
So, crossing Braunau's long extended bridge
And entering Braunau's sentinel-guarded gate,
I said or thought, and waved, a long farewell
To our old comrade many a pleasant day
And many a toilsome, high among the mountains
Or in the déep vales of the north Tïròl.
Our passports viseed — for on Austrian ground
Who sets his foot, had need look sharp to his passport —
And our wine drunk, and not unmerited
Encomium passed upon Hanns Steininger's [1]
Length of beard unexampled — see him, there,
The stately burgher, standing large as life,
Tempera-painted on the southern gate's
Exterior pediment, in his right hand
The imperial patent, at his side, his sword,
The fatal beard down flowing to his feet
In double queue and trailing on the ground
Ominous prodigious — we set out at five,
And, where the road forks at a linden's foot
That, monumental towering there long ages,
Begins at last to bow to stronger Time,
Taking the right hand, and the pine wood entering,
Follow along the dusty, stony road,
Or on the fallen pine-foliage, smooth and slippery,
Our lonely evening way monotonous,
Or varied only by the varying lights
Shed by the golden sunset on the pines'
Red, scaly trunks and cones and dark green needles,
Till the wood opens, and upon the right
Neukirchen shows its tall and taper steeple,
Whither though tired not swerving, but ahead
Pressing with quickened step, we reach ere dark
Dafner's no whit too well kept inn at Dietzing,

---

[1] Bürger, und Magistrats-Rath, der Stadt Braunau. † Sept. 28. 1567. Hat
narrow-brimmed and decorated with a spreading feather.

And, to bed early after early supper,
Exchange this waking motley for sleep's motlier.

Friday, the nineteenth June, returned to earth
From many a visioned flight among the clouds
On wing sublime, or promenade in Eden,
Along brooks rolling orient pearl and gold,
We find our selves, at nine, ripe strawberries culling,
Or luzula's pale insignificant flower,
Or gallant, gay campanulas or phyteumas,
As the pine wood we tread towards Filmannsbach,
And Gundertshausen, where on beer and pancakes,
Setting at nought Hygeia's rules, we dine
In Würzinger's dear inn, and rest a while:
Then forth again at one, and down the hill
Under the Parthenon of the Eggelsberg,
The blessed Virgin's church of the Assumption,
Admiring, at each step, the bold contour
And bearing brave of some Goliath Alp,
The Watzmann it might be, or hohe Goell,
Gaisberg, or Untersberg, or either Stauffen,
Or the pyramidal peak of Sonntagshorn.
Nor wholly without charm of flowers our road:
Orchis, valerian, salvias, tragopogon,
Bicoloured galeopsis, chamomile,
And vicia cracca, centauries and pansies,
Spangle the fields and in the cool east wind
Wave graceful. Lamprechtshausen inn at five
Refreshes us with coffee, and, at seven,
Oberndorf on the Salzach opposite Laufen,
With roast-veal supper, beer, and welcome bed,
All well supplied and cheaply in Kirchgassner's
Honest, unostentatious, brew-house inn.

At half past nine, next morning, up the Salzach,
Oft looking back on Oberndorf's long line
Of houses spread along the green hill's base
And white reflected in the Salzach's blue,
Or on the great dark nave of Laufen church

Peninsular upon the opposite bank
Bavarian. Glowing hot the sun and bright,
Fallen the eastwind that chilled us yesterday.
We leave the road and stretched upon the grass
Bask in the sunshine, Reaumur thirty-three,
In the full rays. Between two rows of oaks,
Through meadows green, our path leads to the water,
And up along the water's rippling edge,
Here bare and sandy, fringed with alder, there,
Cornus sanguinea, and red-blushing roses,
And stately, tall thalictrum's pallid cyme.
On through the wood, then, over the hill's spur,
Where graceful in the oak's broad shadow bends
The turban lily, and wood lysimachia
Expands her tiny yellow petals five.
Emerged, yon 's Salzburg castle on the right
Crowning the hill down in the vale before us,
Distinct, though distant yet some four hour's journey.
Wine and short rest in Anthering at one,
And soon comes into view Maria Plain
Convent and two-towered church the earls of Plain
To mind recalling and good bishop Gandolf
And the blest Virgin's image found unharmed
In the embers' midst, when in the year of grace,
One thousand and six hundred three and thirty,
The swedish heretic laid torch to Regen.
But, on the Heuberg's storm-foretelling top
The white mists gathering, warn us not to loiter,
Nor aside deviate, pilgrims to the shrine
Of the blest Virgin Mother [1], of Good Comfort;
So on, direct, toward Salzburg, where arrived
At half past four, dry-shod, we sup and sleep
Content in our old quarters at the Traube,
Next house to where, upon the very eve
Of finding out the secret which should turn
Death into life, and into gold base metal,
Three hundred years ago died Paracelsus,

---

[1] Maria von gutem Troste.

Philip Aureolus von Hohenheim
Bombastus Theophrastus Paracelsus,
Murdered, they say, why not? for was he not
Reformer and the Luther of physicians,
The overthrower of the papal chair
Infallible of Galen? Ah! if ever
Events on earth occurring touch with joy
Or sorrow the departed, Galen's soul
A thrill of joy felt when it heard in Hades
Einsiedeln's great empiric was no more.

Scarce long enough the next day and the next,
Ancient Juvavium to perambulate,
The colony of Hadrian; from the Mönchsberg
To admire the Salzach threading the white city
With all its minarets and domes squeezed in
Between the Capuzinerberg and Schlossbérg
Yon steeple nearest to thy foot 's saint Peter's
Church of the Benedictines, mausoleum
Of sainted Rupert, Salzburg's holiest dust.
In the sixth century's deepest dark from Worms,
God's messenger, he came; the torch of truth,
Extinguished by the Hunns, relit; the bones
Of Maximus and the fifty martyrs gathered
And covered with a chapel, which, rebuilt
By the fifth abbot Rupert, thou beholdest
Far side the convent, in the graveyard's midst,
Behind the church. Saint Margaret and Saint Amand
Are its two patrons. In the bare rock's side,
Nearer and to the right hand, was his own
Most humble oratory, where all hours
He prayed God to forgive a wicked world
And save his suffering church. First Rupert's Höhle
Then Rupert's Klosterlein they called the place,
And then, for greater honor, dedicated
To Saint Aegidius, and in front of it built
The Kreutz Capelle which from hence thou seest.
Beyond, a narrow stair cut in the rock
Leads painful to Saint Maximus' hermitage.

Ah! those were times when christian priests and bishops
Slept not on beds of down, nor dined off gold,
Nor clothed in crimson velvet and white satin.
That 's Salzburg Dome beyond the Benedictines,
As grand and strong, as fresh and fair, today,
Except some touch of yellow in the marble,
As when, two hundred years ago and forty,
Under Solari's master hand it rose,
At the command of Paris, Count Lodrone,
Salzburg's prince bishop. May it florish long
And long the bones preserve of Saint Vigilius.
That tall lank tower with cupola and ball
The church and cloister shows of the Franciscans.
Airy and light, within, on five free columns,
Hangs the hexagonal presbyterium's vault.
In the year fifteen hundred nine and ninety
Archbishop Wolfgang Dietrich on the Imberg,
(Thenceforward Capuzinerberg called therefore,)
Founded yon cloister of the Capucins
Beyond the river high among the trees.
Now southward turn thine eyes. That's Hohen Salzburg
Crowning the opposite hill this side the river.
There in those strong machicolated towers,
Fearing, alike, and feared, couched in old time
Salzburg's prince bishops, those armed men of God
Who preached, prayed, blessed, judged, punished and absolved,
Enacted and repealed and led to war.
'Twas there mild Leonhard of the golden days
Seized, and in pairs tied, back to back, half naked,
The twenty hapless notables of Salzburg
Who had dared to breathe a faint faint sigh for freedom,
Back to back tied in pairs and dragged on sledges
Half naked under January's frost,
The headsman at their side, to Manterndorf,
And had beheaded, but for the intercession,
Low upon bended knee, of bishop Berthold
Of Chiemsee, and the abbot of Saint Peter's [1]

---

[1] Gerettet starben sie sämmtlich an den folgen der erlittenen misshandlung.
Förster.

Vain intercession; every man, they perished
Killed by the hardship without help of axe.
'Twas there Matthaeus Lang, in fifteen hundred
And five and twenty, in his den shut up,
Defied the rebel boors. 'Twas there Wolf Dietrich
In the next following century's sixth year
Beheaded Casper Vogel and his comrades,
And ten years after died himself, a wretched
Despairing, destitute, detested prisoner.
'Twas there — nay there it is — (above the wall
Thou seest the sentry's shouldered firelock glisten)
Franz Joseph's Croats, lounging by their cannon,
Count, to while time away, how many head
Of Salzburg burghers cross the bridge per hour,
And which more numerous, women, men, or children.
What matter? one well aimed shot sends them all,
Men, women, children, bridge, into the Salzach.
That tumulus half hid among the poplars
Low by the water's edge, on the opposite side
And higher up the river, 's Birgelstein
Few remnants owning now of Roman dust
Or cinerary urns or old Juvavium.
Above, high towering to the clouds, the Gaisberg
Looks down on all — the city and the river,
Castle and dome and convent — and the east
Shuts from the view out. To the south, Pass Lueg,
Distant and blue beyond Hallein and Golling
Admits at once the Salzach to the scene,
And closes to the eye the panorama.

Tuesday, June twenty-third, at half past one
We follow on, despite the gathering storm,
Along the Fürstenweg's gigantic oak
And linden colonnade, our southward journey,
The Salzach on our left, behind us Salzburg,
Before us, parleying with the clouds, Pass Lueg.
Darker the sky each moment, and the wind
More boisterous, and the pelting rain-drops thicker.
And now the gale howls cross the arched allée

Stripping the oak of leaves and twigs, and snapping
Lime branches which come rattling down about us,
Our lives endangering and the path encumbering.
Scarcely we hold our feet, and, with bent knees
And garments fluttering wild before the blast,
Drift insecure, linked mutual arm in arm.
A house stands on our right hand, with its back
Turned to the road and storm; we round the corner,
And under shelter of the front stand cowering,
Safe if the róof hold fast. What noise is that?
A tap upon the window pane invites us,
And through the opening door we enter, thankful,
A ground-floor stube, where a spindle-twirling,
Capless, half-gray, half-bald, lean, wrinkled Sibyl
Bids us be welcome, and we take our seats
On plain deal chairs beside the plain deal table,
Expectant till it please Jove Pluvius
To clear his brow and smile serene again.
A peasant girl, close following on our steps,
The corner of the house rounds, and in haste
Enters the stube, gathers coats, shawls, hats,
Bonnets and shoes, and out again in haste
With both arms full, and rounds again the corner
And disappears. It 's fróm the hayfield she has come;
It 's tó the hayfield she bears much needed help.
And there they come, the haymakers, as drenched
Despite shawls, bonnets, hats, caps, coats and shoes,
As Proteus' sea-calves or as Proteus' self
When at high noon he cómes forth from the waves
And on a rock sits counting up his flock,
Or in a coral cave takes his siesta.
And now the quiet stube 's swarming full,
And noisy as a workshop, and we 're pushed
From seat and table, and look wistful out,
And had almóst preferred the léss rude storm.
Anon the clattering pewter spoons announce
Dinner, that most tyrannical of Gods
Christian or pagan, and, in the table's midst,
A vast, round bowl of coarse, brown earthenware,

Steams like a crater, and, all of a sudden,
One of the rustics, in the hushed crowd's midst
Standing erect, begins to patter prayers,
Which to an end at last come, all sit down —
Some square, some sideways — round about the table
Close packed, and sup their brose cooled with their breath,
Each one his spoon safe ferrying to and fro
With pliant wrist, and elbow on the table
Pivoted. Earnest they are all and silent:
Two have their left arms round their sweethearts' waists.
Emptied the bowl, they 're on their feet again,
And prayers again are pattered, and the stube 's
Again in motion and we 're growing tired,
And the sky 's clearing, and the storm less strong;
So, thanks said to the hospitable spinster,
We brave the road once more and, to the right
Sharp turning, and the gateless avenue entering,
Approach, between two plain stone walls, the royal
Castle of Hellbronn — ill kept residence
Of the Austrian Cesar an odd week in summer —
And the court crossing and by a side door
On the right issuing and upon the left
Leaving the royal Weinschenk, gain again
And follow on the road; and, Anif reached
Ere half past four, lunch economical
In the Obern-wirthshaus, and admire the castle
Elizabethan of the Countess Arco,
With its red flag o'ertopping the red roof
And pointed gables, and reflected gay
In the clear waters of the encircling lake,
Where the swan swims secure, and water-hens
Dip and emerge among the floating lilies.
Our way leads up the valley of the Salzach,
The river on our léft hand, on our right
The Untersberg's steep flank. Beyond the holms
Far side the river, sloping pine-clad hills
Indent the sky with ever varying outline.
Light, feathery clematis, buphthalmum yellow
Cornus sanguinea, privet, harebell blue

And pale euonymus adorn the roadsides.
The equalizing scythe has shorn the fields
Of all their summer glory, leaving only
To sprig the sóft pile of the grassy plush,
Low-creeping nummularia's golden cinquelets.
We cross, and leave behind, the clear, blue Alm
From Berchtesgaden sent down to augment
The Salzach current, strong enough without it
To overset the boat, and deep enough
To swallow at one gulp the seventeen hapless
Churfürstlich brewhouse youths of Kaltenhausen.
It 's eighty years ago, yet not forgot
In Kaltenhausen, that disastrous Sunday,
Nor yet unpitied the diversion-seekers.
At seven we reach Hallein, and for the night
Put up in Grübl's Brauhaus, sup on cutlets,
And go to bed at nine and soundly sleep
Where the green Dürrenberg at once invites
The pious pilgrim to its airy shrine
And strives in vain to hide from prying eyes
And greedy hands, its darkling womb's salt treasures.

Wednesday, June twenty-fourth, "Johannisfest",
We leave Hallein at ten, just as the Halleiners
Refreshed by prayer, come tumbling out of church,
And cross, and, by a path close to the water,
Ascend along the right bank of the Salzach.
Entering the dark pine wood, ere ended yet
The first hour of our journey, we look back
On old Hallein spread out at Dürren's foot
With all its salt pans — Hall and als and Salz
Are but one word, and Salzburg and Hallein
But the more famous and less famous son
Of the same sire — then turn again and onward,
Red and white pine and larch on either hand,
Above our heads the livid tempest lowering,
Not to explode however ere we 're safely
Housed in Schernthaner's, at the Hirsch in Kuchl,
Busy discussing our boiled beef and soup,

And whether only eighteen or quite twenty,
Our landlord's so goodhumored, smiling daughter,
As she pours out our wine and wonders why
We choose to drink it mixed with so much water.
The storm beats on the Rossfeld and clears off,
And now it 's on the Hohe Göll it beats,
And our sky 's bright again, so on through Golling,
And round the tower which closes up the end
Of Golling's street, and up the long steep hill
High on the Salzach's right bank, till aside
Invited by a signpost on our right
To take a peep at Salzach's seething "Kessel".
Helped here and there by friendly rough stone steps
Or uncouth wooden ladder sloping gradual,
Down the precipitous bank we zigzag safe,
To where the fallen-down rocks meet in the midst,
And, jammed together, bridge the torrent over.
We look down through the gaps into the abyss
Where deep below us the impeded waters
Eddy and foam and chafe and thunder through;
Fit washing-house to purge the parted spirit's
Inured guilt, and bleach out the fleshly stain!
Dismal to look down, to look up as dismal.
Dark pines above and spreading beachen shadow
And overhanging rocks almost shut out
The lowering sky and shield us from th' already
For some time pattering rain, but not long shield.
Dripping from every glossy leaf the shower
Begins to wet us, and for shelter drives
Under a rock's eave prominent, to crouch
Squat as two frogs, black hellebore all round
And agaric and lysimachia yellow,
And blue phyteuma, and the snow-white ball
Of opulus viburnum to the ground
Weighed by the rain. Secure we sit in shelter
Where never since the universal flood
Fell one drop water though all round were drowning.
The brightening sky at last, and freshening wind
And solar rays from every dripping leaf's

Diamond-hung point refracting thousand colors,
Invite us forth, and other ladders mounting
And other rough stone stairs precipitous,
We come out on the road high up the Salzach
Opposite a chapel with two limes in front,
Narrow Pass Lueg — Pongau's gloomy portal —
With its strong loop-holed forts right hand and left,
Darkling before us. Not without a shudder
We follow-on our road below the forts,
Along the Salzach's right bank in the bottom,
Oft wondering odoriferous spiraea
Aruncus and sweet harebell and cyclamen
And tiny tophieldia's primrose spike,
Should choose so savage quarters and to live
In Saracen senecio's company
And hardy caltha's and rough barberry's
And crociate gentian's, nor more fear than they
The shade almost perpetual, and keen cutting
Northeast. But lo! first object in the Pongau
Greeting us ere yet crossed the Salzach bridge
To the left bank, a roadside tablet shows
Pictured in every colour of the bow,
How, fifty years ago March twenty-third,
Shot by red-coated Gaul, fell on this spot,
Aged fifty-six complete, Herr Martin Seywald,
And begs one paternoster for his soul,
No word said whether for the public gain
Lawfully, or unlawfully for private,
Was victimized unfortunate Herr Seywald.
The river crossed, Schloss Hohen-Werfen rises
Abrupt before us on its limestone rock,
Towering three hundred feet and seventy-four
Above the perspective diminished waves
Which wash its base, and from the opposite
Taennengebirge [1] separate, where that range

. [1] Tännen (or Jennen)-Gebirge. Ball. Raucheck (7,537') south west corner
of Tännengebirge overlooking Werfen. Ball.

Abuts upon the Salzach. Hohe Kogl [1]
Some, not inaptly some Tiroler Kopf
Call the gaunt peak which clothed with pine below
Hides in the clouds its head, and from its side
Furrowed by torrents, by long ages bleached,
Reflects the slanting sunbeam. Seldom eye
Hath rested on a drearier, lovelier sight.
Eisenhüttenwerk-Werfen's smelting works are passed
And ironfoundry, and our road, deserting
The Salzach for a moment, and ascending,
Passes Schloss Werfen on its rocky spur,
Quadrangular Schloss Werfen with its dwarf
Turrets and loop-hole windows mediaeval,
And battlements and indispensable
Chapel to ease the conscience of its load,
And, on the other side descending, enters
Markt Werfen on the Salzach. The sun sets,
And Night with pallid alchemy reverse,
Turns into copper first, then into lead
The golden coating of Tiroler Kopf.
It is Saint John's feast and by starlight less
Than blaze of hundred Baal fires on the hills
Werfen receives us and not cheaply lodges
In Mühlthaler's bad inn beside the Post,
And with scant supper — bread and wine and pancakes —
Churlish refreshes.

       Half past ten, next morning,
The pair of sluggards sees upon the road,
And, crossed and left behind the Salzach, pressing
Along the Achberg's flank their upward way,
Upward and upward still, till, cleared the comb,
Below them opens trending east and west
The Fritzthal and down hastening to the Salzach
Blue felspath-rolling Fritz, along whose right

---

[1] The Postmaster in Werfen (1868) knew this mountain only by the name of Tiroler Kopf.

And then along whose left bank slow ascending,
Deep between pine-clad precipices dark,
We reach at one the hotel zur Post at Hüttau
Opposite the bare, scald, English-looking church,
And rest a while and lunch on bread and wine
And coffee with vile chicory root embittered,
Then forward up the hill between wide lawns
Blue with campanulas or with ox-eye white,
To Eben, harmless Eben, where we 're not
Even so much as bayed at by the huge
One-headed Cerberus of the hostel door:
Fearless the traveller enters as he lists,
Or fearless passes by — the dog 's of wood;
Sole wooden hostel dog in Germany,
Hostel dog sole in Germany who spurns
The proverb, and his teeth shows without biting.
Therefore I praise thee, Eben! and thy wooden
Cerb, in his wooden kennel with his bright
Collar of brass and heavy iron chain.
And so, without extravagant outlay
Either of valour or of circumspection,
We pass for once a German hostel door,
And have behind us Fritzthal left, and Fritz.
By the Enns watered, flanked upon the east
By Lackenkogel's sugarloaf, the upland
Valley of Flachau opens right before us;
The issuing Enns turns east, and east our road
Turns with the issuing Enns, and on to Radstadt;
Bean fields on either side and chamomile
The air perfuming, and cerinthe minor
And eriophoron with white and yellow
The green holms speckling. Radstadt walls and fosse,
Fosse once, now sunken flower- and kitchen-garden
At six receive us, and with bed and supper
Accommodate, at Poschacher's ill served,
Dear, and not over civil, inn zur Post.

Friday, June twentysixth, at half past eight
We cross the Enns and up the Tauernach's

Right bank pursue our gradual sloping way
Southward, our day's task to ascend the Tauern
And on the further side descend to Tweng —
Pray heaven yon fleecy clouds portend not rain!
A forester with double-barreled gun,
Cock's feather in his hat, and pouch at side,
And spaniel in his steps obsequious trotting,
Joins company, and talks of his revier
And of our journey's pleasures and displeasures,
And how above the level sea our road
To clear the Tauern mounts six thousand feet;
Yet not within one thousand feet and forty
Mounts of the Tauern peak, high Seckar-Spitz.
"Yes, that 's a cembra pine," continued he,
"Rather a rarity among these mountains.
And that 's a prunus padus, rarer still.
And here 's another cembra and another."
"A noble tree 's the cembra pine," said I;
"I saw it first last year near Silva Plana
Upon the Julier, and last year first time
Sang, on my walk from Carlsruhe to Bassano,
Its sturdy Roman air of strength and greatness.
But prunus padus is my old acquaintance,
It grew at Dalkey Lodge upon the lawn
Under my nursery windows, and ofttimes
My childhood sported in the summer mornings
With its white blossoms. Ever since, I 've loved it;
To see it here in this ungenial clime,
These high, cold regions, pains me." With these words
Ended abrupt our talk, for different ways
Our paths led, to the left the forester's
To his revier, mine to our midday halt
Straight onward, at the Unter-Tauern post-house,
Where short our rest, and scanty our repast
Of bread and beer, and forth again undaunted
Under the lowering sky to breast the Tauern,
Leaving the unter-Tauernhaus to flourish
Three hundred years more where it has already
Flourished three hundred, and its portal arch

Display three hundred years more on its key
Sculptured in effigy the wheel of Radstadt,
And date and builder's name and ancestry,
And had we pagans been, we thus had sung:

> Lord of the clouds and murky air,
> Jupiter Pluvius, hear our prayer,
> And graciously this livelong day
> Come not between us and Sol's ray.
> To other shores thy blessings send,
> Bounteous, on other lands descend,
> But from thy servants far away,
> Pluvius Jupiter, keep today.

But not in Jupiter Pluvius or Serene
Was óur faith, or in pagan God or Christian,
But in the good barometer of our host
Of the Unter-Tauern-Haus; so neither song
Nor hymn sang we, nor heaven with prayer assailed.
"Handsome these houses, here, of whole pine trunks
Piled horizontal, one upon another,"
Said I to Katharine, as we left the post house,
"With every one its gable toward the road,
And bell and belfry on the gable's apex,
And white clock-dial, like a Cyclops' eye
Glowering from underneath the prominent
Roof angle, and, below the white clock-dial,
Flower-potted balcony the wide gable's breadth."
But Katharine minded neither white clock-dial,
Belfry, nor bell, nor pine trunks horizontal,
Nor balcony the whole breadth of the gable,
For Flora held her in a flowery leash,
Entangled neck and waist and wrist and ankle,
And with a gentle violence was pulling
Uphill along the Tauernach's right bank.
Of clematis alpina she had wreathed
And calamintha acinos, the garland,
And orange hierácium intertwined
And white pinguicula and geranium phaeum
And chrysosplenium's unobtrusive bloom,
And single flowered erigeron and blue,

Pennoned phyteuma and red sedum repens,
And rock valerian and tall meadow-rue,
And round with cuscuta's long spiral threads
Had wrapped the whole and made into a cord
As strong as it was fair and fragrant smelling.
Such wreath of redder red than her own lips,
Of whiter white than her own teeth, Europa
Twined, sportive, and threw round such willing prisoner,
That fatal day she left the Tyrian shore
For Crete, and little wotting led Jove captive.
Bound with such wreath by Chromis and Mnasylos
And Aegle, loveliest, slyest of the Naiads,
Silenus to regain his liberty
So sweetly sang his song of the creation,
Of Pyrrha, and Pasiphae, and Hylas,
And Atalanta and the golden apple,
And Gallus wandering by Permessus' stream,
That fauns and satyrs gathered round to listen
And forest oaks waved to and fro in time.
As up the steep ravine, far off, I follow,
— The Tauernach below me on the right
Tumbling from rock to rock down toward the Enns,
Upon my left the Kesselwand and Hohlwand
Confining perpendicular the road
And shutting out the sky even to the zenith —
My Muse, seeing me alone, comes laughing up
And links her arm in mine and in mine ear
Sets-to a-flistering such delicious nonsense,
That I hear nothing but herself, see nothing,
Till Katharine's questions: "What kept you so long?
And isn't that Hohlwand fine below the bridge?
And weren't it worth a whole day's pilgrimage
Only to see and hear this waterfall,"
Startle me, and I find myself beside her
Seated high up the left bank of the torrent,
Opposite a cataract whose three cascades
Consecutive fill the air with smoke and thunder,
And hang with spray, trees, rocks, and flowers all round.
But not long time is ours to rest beside

And contemplate the pell-mell of the waters,
For Sol's unceasing, never tiring wheels
Have left, already one good hour and half,
Behind them the meridian, and see yonder,
How down the middle of the road the dust,
Ancient affronts forgiven and forgotten,
Goes pirouetting with old partner Notus,
So onward once again and cross the bridge
So called, of Grace, back to the torrent's right,
And upward round the mountain's rocky spur.
Not without turning oft-reverted eye
On lofty Bischoffsmütze far behind us
Northward, and loftier Dachstein north-north-east,
And upward still, diagonal and upward
Along the slope side of the wooded basin
On whose green level bottom, far below,
The Tauernach meanders toward the Kessel.
Stands on our left a six foot high, time furrowed,
White marble milestone of Septimius Cesar
Severus, carrying back our thoughts across
The chasm of fifteen centuries, till we hear,
And keep time with, the legionaries' tread,
Returning joyous from the Inn's cold banks
Or Danube's to the sunny hills of Tiber.
The basin's brim is cleared and higher still
Along the right of the descending torrent
Winds to the left our road. Up through the larches
Flanking th' abysm below us on our right
Floats louder now and now less loud the roar
Of the Johannis Waterfall unseen.
Following the sound we turn aside where, rubbed
By Time's hand down to scarce four foot in height,
A second stone stands of Septimius Caesar,
And from the chasm's extreme edge contemplate
The Tauernach below and opposite,
Out from the cleft rock's perpendicular face,
Gushing uproarious, and with one brave leap
Plunging, head foremost, down six hundred feet
Into its stony Nesselgraben bed.

Chilly with spray the air; stock, stone, and leaf
Dripping; unsafe the slender, moss grown rail
Which balustrades, two downward steps before us,
The utmost brink. In vain the eye would follow,
Down to the bottom of its fall, the broad,
White, glancing, waving sheet of still new foam.
It disappears and to the ear alone
Sends word of its arrival; every rock
And hollow pine trunk, round, repeats the news.
We turn, and forward up the road again
Under the Hirschwand a Zigeuner group
Descending meets us, women, men and children,
All swarthy, all long-featured, black-eyed all,
And to mind bringing back — though not quite like —
The dark Italian. Some, more in advance,
Have halted, and their temporary camp
Pitched in a green bay of the winding road.
One woman's cooking; one, a little younger,
Sits suckling; from the two-wheeled cart unyoked,
A man, with half bent knee, and hip joint crouching,
Stands motionless before the roadside paling,
His back turned to the road, right hand uplifted,
And bare head and bare neck stretched toward the paling.
Go not too near, disturb him not, he 's — shaving.
A broken piece of silvered glass, his mirror,
Throws the sun's image on us as we pass.
Merry come down the hill, in twos and threes,
His comrades meeting us as we ascend,
And in good German courteously saluting.
We turn when they are passed and stand a while
After them gazing, and in vain some word
Striving to gather of their unknown tongue.
Spangled the roadside grass and edged the brooks
With modest blue forget-me-not and sweet
Unostentatious cowslip and gay trollius,
And vernal gentian and marsh marigold,
And wholesome dandelion, in full bloom,
For, from the lowlands driven by tyrannous Summer,
Spring has ta' en refuge here, and holds, retired,

High on the mountain side, her dewy court,
Under the white mists, and dark, dripping clouds,
Which Sol's warm ray gilds oftener than disperses.
And now ascending higher we have left
Spring and Spring's perfumed, variegated court,
And the soft dropping shower and velvet grass
And tepid slanting sunbeam, far below,
And the breeze nips us and gray mists drift fast
Along the rocky summits, and the rain
Beats in our face, and drips from our umbrellas,
And sky and clouds are blended into one
Opaque, dull, dingy mass of dirty white,
And other garniture our road has none
Than aconite napellus not yet flowered,
Or rhododendron ruddy with the cold,
Or bandy pinus pumilo, or carex,
Or luzula's lank stalk, or chamaebux,
Or Alpine soldanella's blue, fringed bell;
Or, it might be, a patch of livid purple
Silene acaulis, or a squat carline,
Or cineraria crispa scarce half blown,
Or arnica montana scarce half sized,
Or here and there a sally of so dwarf,
Lapland dimensions, that trunk, leaves, and branches
Yield scarce two mouthfuls to the browsing goat,
Or white ranunculus or veratrum album,
Malignant natures both and thriving most
Where kindlier juice and softer fibres die,
And now we 're on the highest of the pass,
The Tauernhorns amphitheatral round us,
Hirschwand and Koppen and Two Mannikins,
And Seekar, rugged all and streaked with snow:
Two hundred yards before us, on our left,
Facing the road, our part desired of refuge,
The Tauernhaus, lone, desolate and naked,
With its white walls and wooden shingle roof,
And windows so to exclude the cold contracted,
And keep the heat in, as to exclude the light
Were ever a cat's pupils: 'cross the road,

Opposite the Tauernhaus, the Tauern church
Wooden, with wooden cross and wooden belfry,
And iron bell with iron tongue to call
The landlord of the Tauernhaus to church:
Close by the dreary church the dreary manse,
Pious foundation of John Wisenegger,
The Schaidtberg's landlord in the year of grace,
One thousand and seven hundred and two score;
Beyond, upon the amphitheatre's verge,
The Tauernhöhe and the Tauern landlord's
Capacious thinly peopled burying ground,
Reigned over in the midst by a Priapus
Christ on the cross, red raddled, gaunt, gigantic,
Terror to thieves, were any on the Tauern,
Or in th' enclosure anything to steal.
At half past three, tired, hungry, wet, behold us
In the grim Tauernhaus' gast-stube seated
Expectant at the bare, brown, walnut table,
Out of a clock-case in the left-hand corner,
Time's everlasting dead-march ticking dull,
A one-wicked lamp, in th' other left-hand corner,
With dismal glimmer lighting in her shrine
A Virgo beatissima soon to be
A Virgo beatissima at once
And mater dolorosa, troubled mother,
Mother of trouble! — for from the stube's low
Swart-raftered heaven, behold in act to fly
Into the lap elite the bridegroom dove.
Nay, uninitiated pagan, nay,
It 's not the repetition of thy Leda.
Blaspheme not, but bow down thy head and worship.
On our right hand the windows and the rain,
A cóld stove at our backs, and, round the stove,
A rail with men-and-women's clothes hung motley;
Against the opposite wall a kneading-trough,
And trough for washing, and huge wooden dresser,
Some half dozen wooden platters on the shelves
And twice as many quart and pint, bright shining,
Beer-glasses, with bright polished pewter lids

54

Hinged on, and standing open and each bearing,
Our host's initials in fair graven letters,
At last before us smokes upon the table
Th' expected scheiterhaufen, and we dine
Not without thoughts of Dido, and drain, each,
Our foaming pint of beer, then, satisfied,
And, as in duty bound, to Ceres, thankful,
And cordial, kind Gambrinus, forth again
Under the clearing sky at half past four,
And, left behind the burying-ground and cross
And, cleared the Tauernhöhe, feel not sorry
That now, at long and last, the road leads downward,
Downward leads gradual, snowdrifts on our right
And dark slate rocks. white marble, on our left,
Coarse, dolomitic, little like the fine
Hard, homogeneous Carrara block
Or snow-white Parian; high above our heads
On either hand the bare cliffs thinly sprinkled
With stunted larch or spruce, the skyish zenith
Now overcast, now clear, and now, again,
Raining; Reaumur plus eight, roads wet, streams full,
And, lower down as we descend, gold-edged
With marigold or fringed with saracen
Cacaglia not yet blown, nor hoisting yet
Upon its slender scape its purple-red
Umbrellula, and heath begins to bloom
·And primula farinosa and elatior,
And stalkless gentian and bavarica,
And bilberry, and white Idaean vine,
And heart-leafed globularia, gray and sad,
And we bid fárewell to the last dwarf sally.
Deep down below us on our right, the valley
Grassy and green, as, under the pine wood
Now thicker grown upon the heights above us,
We wind along the left-hand mountain flank.
And see and hear the torrent underneath
The bridge of Hoheberg dashed into foam
Whiter than the white marble rocks. Down still
Our road leads gradual, and — behind us leaving

Farther and higher at each step the Tauern's
Bare, rugged, snow-streaked ridge, and on the left
Passing a pair of five-foot-high, time-worn
Gray milestone columns of "Invincible,
Imperial Philip, Cesar and Augustus,
And Tribune of the people", — lands us safe,
At half past seven, in the post house at Tweng,
Where a veal-cutlet supper, beer, and salad,
And tolerable beds, and long sound sleep,
Leave us no word to say against the Tauern.

    June Twentyseventh wears of his elder brother,
June Twentysixth, the fashion; clouds and rain
Diversified with patches here and there
Of sunshine and blue sky. Tweng left behind,
We follow on alert, at nine o'clock,
With the descending Tauern stream, our way;
Smooth polished, various colored pebbles glancing
Bright through the ripple, underfoot, the sward
Though wet, elastic; and, about us round,
Green barberry in full canary bloom,
And feathery larch the torrent's left bank clothing,
Not enough thick to make our path swerve often,
Or often from our view shut out the ripple. _
And now we 've changed for the high road the sward,
And, for vast heaps of rusty iron gravel,
The barberry blossom pale, and feathery larch;
And clattering foundry hammers stun our ears,
And the Tauern torrent's busy turning wheels
Some under-shot some over-, and we tread
Crisp scoriae, and a sulfurous glow Etnaean
Steams in our faces as we pass the furnace,
And naked armed and naked legged stalks here
A sweating Steropes, a Brontes there,
A swart Pyracmon yonder, and sparks fly
In their old fashion upwards, and smoke wreaths
Hang in the air, and soot begrimes the portals.
Lovelier see now before us — on the green
Larch-studded knoll that toward the river crowns

Th' extreme end of the spur cross which the road,
Ascending first, descends to Mauterndorf —
Mauterndorf castle with its Gothic loop-holes
And square, white, massy tower a hundred feet
And forty, high, above the courtyard pavement.
Arrived, an hour ere Sol from his meridian
Peeps through a cloudy chink on Mauterndorf,
We dine luxurious on boiled beef and salad,
And praise the landlord's year-old Styrian wine,
And provident memorandum in our tablets:
"Opposite the church, Post good in Mauterndorf."
And, rested, on again, at prick of noon,
Along a dull, monotonous road between
Flax and rye fields, these purpling, those in bell,
Not without now and then reverted eye
On Mauterndorf, and Mauterndorf's white castle
Standing forth in the sunbeams bold and fair
Against the larch-clad mountain's dark back-ground;
Nor without farewell and a pleasant journey
Waved from the bridge down to the Tauern stream
Here parting company and turning east
To join the Mur at Tamsweg; onward then
Over the Staigberg's spur, and all at once
Between the Mitteberg and Staigberg opens
The Mur's green valley trending west and east
From Saint Michaèl to Tamsweg; Mosham Schloss,
Honored scarce less as Bierschenk than as Schloss,
Close at our feet; Saint Margaret's opposite.
Westward, our down-hill road ascends the Mur
To Saint Martìn, where a gendarme accosts us,
In German, plainly not his mother tongue,
Though fluent spoken. He 's a Milanese
With full, dark, melting, mulberry eyes Italian,
And sallow, pompion cheeks: three years he has spent,
Three long sad years, here in this Alpine eyrie,
Out of the sound of "sì sì" and "buon giorno".
Learning to chew black bread, and with long draughts
Of glutinous córn-wine lubricate his throat,
With *ichs echs ochs* and *achs* made sore and husky.

I never had much sympathy with gendarmes,
Not even in old dear Dublin where they drilled me
As if they had been drill sergeants, I, a raw
Awkward recruit; and high up in the mountains
Among the cembra pines and rhododendrons
A gendarme is my horror and disgust.
What! shall not I, who to no mán mean harm,
Who would not hurt a fly, or even so much
As brush down wantonly a spider's web,
Shall I not tread the mountain sod unquestioned?
And sleeps the Austrian Kaiser insecure
Unless by telegraph transmitted to him,
Each night before he goes to bed, my doings?
How many miles I' ve walked to day, how many
I intend to walk tomorrow, where I 've dined
And slept and baited, and the hour precise
I left my last night's quarter? and should ever
A doubt rise in thy mind, inquisitive reader,
Of the stern truth of all this travel's story,
Thou canst at pleasure verify names, dates,
And all the principal facts, by reference
To the imperial archives in Vienna.
I never had much sympathy with gendarmes
Yet I felt for the man and bade him kindly
"Addio!" when, arrived at Saint Michael,
He touched his cap and turned into the guardhouse.
Across the Mur our left-hand-veering road
Conducts us now, and we begin to ascend
The steep side of the Katschberg, stopping oft
To dráw breath and look back upon the valley,
River, and Saint Michael, and the opposite hill
Of Pfaffenberg, renowned for its fair prospect,
And Speiereck's cloudy Spitz pyramidal.
Open our road at times, at times closed in ·
By larch or pine woods, never not deep furrowed
By many a crossing mountain stream oblique,
Or mountain stream's bed, and ascending ever
Steeper and more abrupt than even the Tauern,
But to less height. We 're on the top at six,

And, with one stride the Lungau left behind,
Enter Carinthia, of all lands we 've travelled,
— For not now for the first time do our feet
The soil tread "where the rude Carinthian boor
Against the houseless traveller shuts his door" —
The least polite to strangers. No less steep,
No less by streams deep furrowed the descent,
No less the view, than in the ascent, shut out
By larch and pine woods and revealed alternate.
On all sides round decaying mica-schist,
Below us on the right the Pölla thal
And from the Hafner hasting down to meet us
Through the pine wood, the Lieserbach at Rennweg;
Offside the valley, rising high before us,
And closing in the prospect, the obtuse
Cone of the Wandspitz; on the left below us
Rennweg, not yet in view, but safely reached
At half past seven. Our lodging 's in the Poste.
Our supper, chicory, salad, veal and beer,
Our landlord's Joseph Heiss, as pope or Cesar
Potent in Rennweg, and, with pope's or Cesar's
Abhorrence of imperium in imperio,
Safe centering in himself the powers that be
In Rennweg — burgomaster sole, sole landlord,
Sole master, both of letter-post and horse-post.
Beware him, traveller — happy, if thou canst,
And need'st not even for one night trust thyself
To Rennweg's irresponsible dictator.
We need it — woe to need and ignorance!
Ignorance, bad father; Need, unhappy son.
Supper despatched, bed-chamber-candles waiting
Lit on the table, "Passports, please", said Heiss,
With outstretched arm between us and the door,
Obstructive. Even as ticket-of-leave man humbly
Takes out and shows his ticket, I take out
And show our noble Queen Victoria's letter
Praying all foreign princes, potentates,
Thrones, dominations, virtues, her fair cousins,
To afford us two, her peaceful, loyal subjects,

Free and safe passage through their several realms,
Small courtesy, with like small courtesy
To be by her in similar case requited:
"Is 't not enough?" said I, seeing Heiss demur;
"Go up" said he, "leaving with me the passport."
"Your part 's to read," said I, as in my pocket
I buttoned up the document, "and object
If you find aught wrong; mine 's to keep the passport.
"How do I know," said he "but in the morning
My guest goes off at cockcrow, scot unpaid?"
"I 'll pay you now," said I, "make out your bill,"
And down upon the table laid the money.
"But there are chairs and tables, in the room,
Besides the beds and bedclothes; who secures me
To find them or my guests tomorrow morning?"
Then put a sentinel on our door," said I,
"And guard us well, for not except by force
Touchest again our passport. Good night, landlord."
"Landlord, good night", said Katharine, and both turning
Short on the heel round, took up each a light
And up to bed, leaving Heiss there surprised
And hesitating and no word heard more
Of pledge or passport, and in sound sleep, soon,
And dreams of happy home and kindly faces,
Forgot inhospitable, rude Carinthia.

At half past seven next morning Reaumur stands
At twelve within our chamber, from the north
The wind blows steady, and before it drives
In troops across the sky the lazy clouds.
Our way leads down the valley of the Lieser
Crossing from bank to bank oft, and recrossing;
Larch and pine forests clothe on either hand
The heights above us; granite rocks detached
Lie round about us; over rounded pebbles
Of quartz and granite rolls the clear cold stream.
Roofless and cracked and ruined are the walls
Of ancient Rauhenkatsch signorial castle
High on its grassy knoll upon our right,

Above the Lieser out of the ravine
From behind rushing, and our downward way
Unceremonious crossing; but the bridge,
Though crazy, holds fast, and we pass secure
Where Joseph Martin Kulnigg, his imperial
And royal Highness's road engineer,
Fell with seven masons through the half finished arch,
And, by the swollen flood swept away, had perished,
But for the help, invoked upon the instant,
Of Malta chapel's *Mary of all comfort*.
Graved letters on the parapet preserve
Already for one hundred years less four,
The memory of the fact. Incessant raves
The Lieser at the foot of Rauhenkatsch,
Incessant echoes, opposite, the ravine's
Schistose gneiss rock, with mingled birch and larch
And dark red pine, thick wooded to the clouds.
And see on yonder weather-beaten ledge,
Above the road beyond the bridge and river,
Stands tenantless a blood-stained cross with spear
Nail-holes and leaning ladder; underneath,
Chiselled out in the precipice's face
And by a steep stone stair accessible,
The tomb yawns transverse of a ghastly, pallid,
Full length extended, dead, white-sheeted Christ.
Sprinkled the corpse with gilly-flower and rose,
And, round the opening's sill, blooms fresh and fair,
Cared by some pious hand, a boxed-in plat
Of wall-flower, pink, and lily-of-the-valley.
Who reads unmoved the scroll upon the lintel,

Christians, come if ye love Jesus
And hold sacred his command,
From the heaven of heavens he sees us
Reverent kneel and kiss his hand. —[1]

[1] Christen! rührt euch Jesu liebe,
Ist euch heilig sein geboth,
O! so kommt aus reinem triebe,
Kommt und feiert seinen tod.

Is of less plastic clay made than the crowd.
Downward along the Lieser, downward still
Leads on, our road, the gneiss rock on our right
Green here and there with elder racemose,
And mountain-ash in flower, and barberry;
Upon our left the torrent, overhead;
Firm on the perpendicular cliff's edge,
The village and white church of Nikolai,
Cynosure of the valley, but we turn
Forward direct our undevotional eyes
And hastening steps alert, and at Kremsbruck,
Peninsular between the Krems and Lieser,
Crossing the Lieser, first, and then the Krems,
And then the blended waters, dine at two
In Bürgermeister Kolmeyer's inn, in Gmünd,
And rest an hour, then cross the Malta bridge,
And stand by, witness of the joyful meeting
Of the two Alpine sisters undefiled,
Malta and Lieser, and, upon their journey
Down to Spitàl to meet their cousin Drau,
Accompany as far as Lieserhofen
The united pair, not with them, hand in hand,
Leaping from rock to rock along the deep
Ravine's rough bottom, but, with even step
And sure along the smooth, fair road that crowns,
And in and out winds with the bosky brink,
And looks down from above, through birch and ash
Willow and flowering elder on the water,
And, cross the water, on the opposite bank's
Willow and birch and ash and flowering elder.
But Lieserhofen parts us from our comrades;
They toward Spitàl right on; toward Lendorf we;
To the right turning at the crucifix;
Shorter our way so, by th' hypothenuse,
Than through Spitàl and the sharp angle's vertex,
And we shall gréet Drau ere she has met her cousins.
Fair spreads and wide the view from Lieserhofen,
Down the Drau valley east towards Klagenfurth
And nearer Villach, though the Drau's unseen,

Unseen the Millstadt lake and town of Millstadt
Hid in the lower heights and jutting spurs
O'er which our eye expatiates unconfined
Eastward — "but what is that you 've got there, Katharine,
So glossy black, soft, plump, and velvety,
With so great massy paws and eyes no bigger
Than a pin's head?" "A little mole, papa.
Never before this day alive by me
Beheld the tiny, timid, rapid miner."
"Let him go, Katharine, and if death's his portion,
For doing that which he must do or starve,
Let us to other hands the execution
Leave of fell Nature's stern, Draconian law;
Us he has never harmed." "And him, be sure,
I have no thoughts of harming," answered Katharine,
As, at his own door, she set free her prisoner,
And, sympathizing, watched his disappearance.
At half past six behold us facing West
Up the wide bottom of the great Drau valley,
Right in the wind's eye. Treeless, shrubless, hedgeless,
The bleak, flat, dusty road; maize on our right,
Upon our left hand, maize; unseen, beyond
The left hand, maize; the river cuddling in
Close to the southern mountain's barren base.
Black, black the sky to the southwest before us,
And, from the mountain flank on which it lowers,
Not by unpractised eye to be distinguished.
Under that heavy, leaden, lowering sky,
Behind that mountain's spur, lies Sachsenburg,
Our three-miles-distant refuge for the night,
And we must turn oblique from the northwest
And setting sun, in state, and Möll's bright valley.
Desolate Möllbrücken village; clear and cold
From the Great Glockner and Pasterzen-Kees
Under its wooden bridge flows down the Möll,
And seeks the Drau out hid behind the maize,
Coy as a maid who nought will hear of marriage.
Our way to Sachsenburg both rivers crosses
And the acute peninsula between,

And in Kapeller's inn and bakery
Lodges us safe for supper and the night,
And the dark, leaden, lowering sky may now
Descend in rain or clear up, as it likes.

Saint Peter and Saint Paul a windy day
Have for their festival, June twentyninth,
And Notus in our face his heavy wings
Flaps disrespectful, as, at ten o'clock,
We cross from Sachsenburg the wooden bridge
And up the left bank of the Drau press, lively,
Through the pine wood, where, of its honors shorn,
Each once majestic pine no worthier shows
Than a lank maypole or pyramidal poplar.
But need's no less imperious than sharp witted
And where to bed the cattle there's no straw,
Or little, the pine bough must serve the purpose:
Nor to the Goddess of the turret crown
Let the fate hard seem of her protegee;
Have not philosophers' and poets' pages
And the historian's hard wrought, learned volumes
Heated the public baths and baking ovens
Of mighty Alexander's famous city?
Who 'd tread the dusty road when at his side
A grassy path runs parallel, strewed with fern
And pungent juniper and ripe strawberries?
And now our way grows swampy, and green frogs
Plash from beside our feet into the water,
And blue libellulas with expanded wings
Flitting before us, challenge to give chase.
But we prefer a less fugacious game,
And cull, at every step, some painted blue
Or red recruit, or yellow, for our nosegay,
Sanguine anchusa, mullein tall and stately,
Soft eriophoron, and forget-me-not,
And fragrant-blossoming elder, and spiraea,
And tunica saxifraga, and humble
Roadside convolvulus, and wholesome mallow,
And barberry's green leaf and yet green berries,

And chicory here first in flower this journey —
Cheap and vile counterfeit of the Arab berry, —
And broad-disked daisy and chrysanthemum
Emulous of Juno's full, resplendent eye,
And lychnis pink and lychnis white, and carex;
And purple centaury, and woodbine yellow
And garnish all round with red blushing roses,
And with green pteris aquilina sheathe
And bind with bindweed; fairer nosegay never
Laid Flora's votary at her goddess' feet.
In and out with the mountain's bays our road
Winding ascends along the Drau's left bank,
And not unfrequently in sheltered nook
The sunny sward to sit and rest invites us
Not loath, for sick and weak, to day, my comrade,
All other days so lively, strong. and active,
And than myself more patient of the way's
Manifold hardships: nor, dearest Katharine, ever
Till I 've forgotten thee and thy not soon
To be forgotten mother, shall my heart
Or tongue or pen subscribe the narrow creed
That woman is a creature less than man
Endowed with fortitude and perseverance —
"Less strong, sir poet," to be sure, less strong.
But not inferior therefore, unless man's
Inferior to the ox. "Less rational" —
Be it so, reasoner, whom unreasoning woman
Circumvents at her pleasure. Salomon, Sampson,
Coriolanus, witness. True that Juno
Hearkened sometimes to Jove, but Jove himself,
With all his thunders and with all his oaths,
What was he but the minister most humble
Of the weird sisters' all-ordaining will?
But let that pass, for, breasting us, behold
Th' accumulated gravel broad and high
Which Steinfeld torrent, in long lapse of ages,
Has carried with it from the mountain down,
And spread out for its own hard pebbly bed.
Oblique, as if to spare my comrade's strength,

Our road ascends, and on the other side
Oblique descends to Steinfeld where, at three,
In the new-wirth's inn — first house on the left —
Premature stopping for the day, we dine
And the long evening lounge, then sup and sleep.

Tuesday, June thirtieth, Reaumur in our chamber
Stands at eighteen; outside the wind blows fresh
Down the Drau valley; clear the sky of clouds,
And of clouds clear our minds, and to Hygeia
For a long night's sound sleep, restorative
Of health to Katharine, to us both of strength, —
Both of us thankful. Bless us still, Hygeia,
Thou who alone mak'st life a gift worth having
Even to the immortals, thou of Gods above
And Gods below and men held in like honor.
At ten we 're on the road, green wheat all round us,
Barley in ear, and long rye turning yellow,
And flax in bell, and beans the air perfuming,
And stately, tall, green maize, and purple flowering
Lurid potato. Noon beholds us scaling
With longer stride and firmer foot to day
The Knopnitz delta up to Greifenburg
High on its eastern glacis, crossing then
The Knopnitz torrent proud to have for its own
Sole use and profit, like the Persian despot,
Lowered the mountain and the valley raised,
Then down the western delta flank descending
Into the midst of pear and apple orchards,
Walnut and cherry and white-flowering elder
Balsamic, and blue linten fields, sweet contrast
To the gray, barren, gravelly delta's waste.
Carinthian women comely-featured, tall,
And well proportioned, in blue cotton skirts
And sleeveless bodices and white shift sleeves,
And ruddy arms bare from the elbow, meet us,
Carrying rakes on their shoulders; and the gay
Song of haymakers and fresh smell of hay
Greet us right hand and left. And now again

Ascent laborious of another delta
Bearing its parent torrent on its shoulders —
Aeneas-like, — gigantic, aboriginal
Pine-studded aqueduct of granite pebbles
And quartz and mica-schist. And on the left,
Drau, hid since Greifenburg, comes into view,
And wooden bridge across; and winter snow
Lies pale and ghastly in the southern mountains'
Cold, sunless, joyless, dolomitic clefts.
Berg on the right passed on its slope above us
And, on the left, a rustic roadside scroll '
Showing how, on his home return to Linth,
John Winkler on this spot fell from his cart,
And underneath the heavy laden wheel
Ended, abrupt, his earthly joys and sorrows.
You see him there face downward in the dust,
The wheel upon his neck and, from the clouds
Pitiful looking down, the maiden blest.
Midway, the disembodied soul flies upward,
As like John Winkler as a twin to his brother,
Or photograph or waxwork to the model.
Dellach at three, and lunch of bread and wine,
And half an hour's rest, and some human pity
For a Hungarian traveller on his way
To native Arad from the eternal city.
He tired, poor lad! of clarifying sugar
All the long day in Arad, and broke bounds,
And breathed with joy, a roving journeyman,
New air in Frankfort on the Main and Hamburg,
And crossed the sea from Cette, and from Jerusalem
The desert, to the Babylonian frontier,
And has made sugarcandy in Grand Cairo.
And now, his father dead, there 's waiting for him
In Arad, he doubts not (who doubts at twenty?)
His patrimony of six thousand florins
And his pale cheek glows red, and dark eye glistens
As he counts up how many days to Arad.
Ritterdorf's roadside hostel greets us next,
And by a Turk's head, pipe in mouth, surmounted

A fountain opposite and grassy seat,
And merry group of damsels Tyrolese,
The cool enjoying of a flowering linden's
Sacred, wide spreading, odoriferous shade,
And red-lead painted, twenty-foot-high cross,
With all its grisly garniture, nails, thorns,
Spear, hammer, pincers, ladder, sponge and cock,
And grim, dead God. Another delta then,
Torrent and alders; and, as we descend,
Some stately onopordons, whether native
Or from a garden strayed, no vulgar race.
High on the mountain's breast, beyond the river,
We leave behind conspicuous Schloss Stein
And its white chapel, and in Ober-Drauburg
Halt at the Ober-lieutenant's for the night,
Sure of good quarters and a kind reception
From our old friend the landlord of the Rössle;
And from our windows hear the rush of Drau.

Sound sleepers may be robbed anights; we weren't:
Sound though we slept last night; or, still worse case,
Wake, as we woke this morning, to be told
How by a few short hours we have missed the rarest
Of high Heaven's condescensions to low man,
Ocular demonstration of a miracle;
For the All-Wise, at long and last deferring
To Ober-Drauburg's prayers and reclamations,
Changed hand, last night, and to his ill-considered,
Untimely drought an end put with a shower,
And now all's right again in Ober-Drauburg,
And votes of thanks were passed last night at midnight,
And churchbells rung, and deputation sent
Of priests and notables to Maria Hilf,
Acknowledging the favor, and for ever
Vowing adhesion to a government
Wise in its very nature and unerring;
Yet not the less on that account disposed
To listen to and square its conduct by
The will and pleasure of its erring subjects;

Let it but be respectfully expressed,
And urged home with undoubting faith and fervor.
But when we wake next morning, if we 've missed
The demonstration, we 've at least not missed
The miracle's self; it rains on Oberdrauburg
With such miraculous rain as upon us
It has rained every day since we left Salzburg.
By the blue sky assured, at half past twelve,
That, their turn served, the Oberdrauburgers
Have sent the deity about his business,
We pack up, bid good bye, and to the road
Between pyramidal poplars; on our right,
High on the Alpine hip, the castle gray
Of Rosenberg; Maria Hilf beyond,
White in the sheltered nook; upon the left
The Drau, irreverent, carrying to the sea
The miracle of last night. Behind us lie
At two p. m. the frontier of Tirol,
And Nikolsdorf, first town, and on our view
Opens the fair wide basin of Lienz,
Rendez-vous joyful of the mountain nymphs
Isel and Drau, that from the Dreiherrnspitz
And Great Venediger's everlasting ice,
This from green Toblach's watershed descending.
Dolomite peaks upon the south keep guard,
Lasertzwand and Hochkempen and Spitzkofel
And high Hochstadl, bleakest of the Unholde.
Miraschist Schleinitz opposite rears high
Toward the northwest his barrier, on the east
And just behind us left, stands sentinel
Ridged Ziethen and looks westward toward Lienz,
Close at the Schlossberg's foot peninsular
Between the valleys of the Drau and Isel.
South, on the basin's lower, inner inn,
Lias Rauchkofel's wooded pyramid,
And the Kirschbaumeralp to botanists dear,
And Zabarott's shapeless lump, upon the north
And our right hand, the prospect shutting in
And turning rude the back upon the Moelthal

And Boreas' proffered kisses, Iselberg,
Zetterfeldberg, the Stronacher, and Gaimberg,
With all their deltas, torrents, and ravines,
Green, smiling, velvet slopes and rough plush forests,
And wooden houses, separate or in groups,
And churches raising high to heaven the honored,
Never enough to be respected, cross.
Gravelly and rough the field each side the road,
The short coarse grass with mountain clover sprinkled,
And carex ampullacea always near
The stream's side and white sedum on the wall,
And, strange contrasting with marschantia's brown
Glutinous blotch, the delicate canary
Blossom of hieracium pilosella
And blood stained orobanche battens on
Spicy-breathed thymian's root; and hare-bell droops
Modest, and with gauze net, compassionate,
Pea-green selaginella clothes the ground.
And not alone shrub barberry, Tirol's
Dearest, most cherished child, adorns the deltas,
But stateliest verbascum mingles there
Its yellow blossom with stramonium's white,
And dulcamara round the alder's branch
Swings herself pliant, and solanum swart
Hides himself conscious in the shade behind.
Passed on the right the Wirthshaus zum Capaun
And Dölsach church and village, and the road
Thrice by us trod in old times, three years since,
Descending from the Glockner to Lienz,
What time we crossed, without or path or guide,
In ten long hours, the lofty Fuscher-Tauern,
Feat hardly by the sane to be attempted;
And five years since, when by this Pusterthal
Taking our way from Milan to Vienna
We turned aside and slept one night at Dölsach —
And passed upon the left the holms where pines,
Torn from its Alpine home by summer floods,
And forced to colonize a soil ungenial,
The noble edelraute, and — far off

In the Lasertzwand's shade beyond the Drau —
The hill of Lavant passed, upon the left,
With its two churches, Peter's-and-Saint-Paul's
High on the summit, half way up Saint Ulrich's,
Both sacred, but Saint Ulrich's sacred most,
Shrine of the Virgin who in glory here
Appeared not to the shepherds but the sheep,
And by the whole flock, wedder, ewe, and ram,
On bended knee, was worshipped. Passed at last
The old dismantled bildstöckl and hand
Gracious uplifted in the act to bless,
And crossed the Isel bridge, and left behind
The wretch's last sad refuge, the spitàl,
We reach Lienz at four and in the Post,
Often before tried and found never wanting,
Put up, and from our windows, pleased, look out
Upon the sun-lit platz and the Lienzers,
And Liebburg Schloss, Lienzer court house now,
More than three hundred years ago the proud
Residence baronial of the Wolkenstein
Rodeneck, Freiherrn of the Drau and Isel,
After Graf Leonhard, the last earl of Görtz,
Had for red marble tomb in Saint Andrae
Exchanged Schloss Bruck, and, for a heavenly crown,
The lordship of the Drauthal and the Isel.

    Two days pass lightfoot by, whilst, in old Loncium
— Roman post-station once upon the route
From Aquileia to the Bridge of Oenus —
We wait until the weather, put about
By th' Oberdräuburg miracle, has resumed
Temper, and pharmacopolist Franz Keil
Collated our Reaumur with the exact one
Of the barometer sent him from Vienna
For his new reckoning of the Glockner's inches,
And given us lessons in the Drauthal flora
Each evening and each morning, and excursion
Botanical made with us to Schloss Bruck
And Leopoldsruhe, and we have spent two hours

In admiration of his isohypsish
Drawings, and plaster model of the Glockner,
All with his own hands measured, drawn, and colored;
Nor deign we not, though heretics, a visit
To the Madonna of the Heimsuchung,
Less, the plain truth to tell, out of devotion
Than to see Dusi's famous altarpiece
And hear the fair Dominicans sing vespers,
We the sole auditors, if you except
Saint Horian's statue on the Gospel side,
And on the Epistle's, holy Nepomuck's,
And, in the clouds, above the vaulted roof,
Such Gods and angels as have time to listen,
And ears have for plain vocal *do re mi*,
Unhelped by organ, lute, or even a whistle.
The church of Saint Andrae, beyond the Isel,
Beguiles us of an hour, too, with 'ts red sculptured
Leonhard last Earl of Görz,[1] and Gothic porch —
And Lombard — lions they may be or griffons —
And flowering linden tall — of pyramids
Gracefullest — and snug pfarrhof alongside.

And so, almost before we are aware,
Comes the third day, all shining bright and glowing,
And not one cloud deforms the Schleinitz Spitz,
Or of its full nine thousand feet and nine
Abates one inch. At ten, our luggage packed
And sent to await us at Conegliano,
And letters posted for our Carlsruhe friends,
Chronicling faithful all our roadside marvels,
We bid good bye, and take across the fields
The path to Leisach, on our left the Drau,
Upon our right above our heads the bowers
And baths and mineral springs of Leopoldsruhe.
Except our foot-tread and the rush of Drau,

---

[1] Leonhard last Earl of Görz is on the left immediately after you enter the church. Wolkenstein and his wife in similar red marble on right, directly opposite him. Since our former visit both monuments have been removed from the Presbytery to this situation where they are in the dark and escape observation. J. H. 1865.

In the Lienzer Pass no sound is heard,
Where eight and forty years ago — come winter —
Every scaur, either side the road, re-echoed,
And every bush, the Pusterthaler's rifle,
And every echo was a Frenchman's knell.
The Auerwirth with dinner entertains us
At half past one, and shows us in the Au
The tablet on the spot raised where young Jacob
Vergeimer from his horse fell on the seventh
September, forty nine, and, dying sudden,
Went straight to heaven without paraphernalia,
Defrauding church and college of their dues,
And licensed neither by red gown nor surplice.
"Ah, wretched!" said the Auerwirth, meaning, wretched,
To die without being shrived; "alas, most wretched!"
We answered, meaning to put faith in shriving,
And no less from the truth far, than the Auerwirth,
For, lo! enthroned in clouds heaven's maiden queen
— How different maiden queen from England's Bess,
Of how much less inflexible hard heart,
Bear witness thou, sweet Bethlehem innocent —
Baby in lap, and gold crown on her head,
— I quote the right hand corner of the picture,
For who not sees the fact must with the next
Best evidence content him — stretches forth
Her right hand towards Vergheimer, bids him welcome,
And take his seat within the blest purlieus,
Near, but not in, the first row of the saints,
Near, but not in, the full light of th' Eternal.
Mittewald post-house left behind and crossed,
To the right bank, the Drau, and to the left
Recrossed beyond the pine wood, we ascend,
And on the other side descend, while Drau
Goes round about Abfalterbach's steep hill,
Between flax fields in bell and black-eyed bean,
And lóng rye, blighted by the frosty night
Of June fifteenth: we spent that night in Winzer,
Reader, thou mayst remember, and, next morning,
Saw every blade hoar with the fatal spar.

And not alone in high Abfalterbach
But wide through North Tirol and all Carinthia,
To day, July the fourth, the premature
Despairing sickle reaps the earless straw,
And winter's wind shall pipe through empty garners.
Time was when neither Drau went round about,
Nor traveller up and down, the delta steep
West of the village of Abfalterbach,
But both went friendly side by side along
The straight and level bottom, not as yet
Had Messa lake broke barrier and borne down
Into the bottom, Messa and Messaners,
And half the faithless clay-slate mountain side;
And Strassen was not yet, nor Strassen church,
Nor the flax fields, or rye, or black-eyed bean,
Poppy, or buskined buckwheat, which to day
Flank our ascending and descending road
Over the delta of Abfalterbach.
And now alongside overflowing Drau's
Half-reclaimed marsh, our road runs level on
Under the right-hand steeps to Panzendorf
And Heimfels castle beetling overhead,
Villgraten torrent rushing noisy by,
And, crossed the covered bridge, at Sillian lands us
Safe in the comfortable Post at seven.
The landlord recognizes us, we sup
On soup, wine, omelet, apricots, and cherries,
And soundly sleep, and wake betimes, next morning,
Out of dim visions philological
Of Heimfels, Heunfels, Hunnenfels and Hun,
And loop-holed stones inserted in tower walls
To admit the light and let the arrow out.
Or, maybe, it is Cynthia's beam pours in
Upon some sleeping, pious, Hun Eneas,
Showing him, face and ribboned hair revealed,
His Hun Penates at his bedside standing,
And warning not to settle on the Drau,
But up and take them with him to Friuli —
And sweat, outbursting, proves it is no dream.

And then, our vision changing, giant Hano
Of Toblach brandishes the bloody rib,
And Heimfels changes masters, and we awake
In Silian post house and, look out on Heimfels'
Keep and embattled wall and loop-holed towers
Crowning the steep, dark rock, and, what though gray,
Time worn and wrinkled, showing fresh and fair
In the new risen sun's all enlivening ray.
Nor without all respect do we salute
On the same rock watch-keeping, by the same
Impartial beam beneficent illumined,
Lying Saint Peter's church, and, in the shade,
Saint Antony's below, and Panzendorf,
And the Villgraten torrent rushing by
Under the covered bridge to join the Drau
Down in the bottom posting to the Euxine.

　　Sunday, July the fifth, at half past nine
We 're on the road, Reaumur at plus thirteen,
The sky without a cloud, the weather settled,
Silian behind us eastward, to the west
The upper Pusterthal before us rising.
Peasants, from Silian's morning mass returning,
Keep pace beside us and the road enliven,
And eye us no less curious than we them.
The men wear green cloth jackets and a green
Cock's feather in their conical green hat.
Green worsted girths outside the vest suspend
Black cotton-velvet breeches, at the knee
Unbuttoned, and below the knee exposing
Above the gartered stocking the tawn skin:
Shod with laced leather boots the feet and ankles;
The brawny calf distends the snow white stocking,
A leathern girdle broadening to the front
Narrowing behind, and with split peacock quill
Gaily embroidered, in the midst displays
Th' imperial eagle, or the wearers' name,
A *gems*, or other rural coat of arms.
The women's similar conical felt hat

75

Instead of feather bears a gold lace band,
And gold-lace tassel. Of black cloth the gown
Long sleeved, short waisted, tight at wrist and shoulder,
Wide at the elbow; the deep-plaited skirt
Too short to hide the polished shoe's rosette,
Or clocks of the white stocking, far too short
To tether in the mountain maiden's step,
And in Tiról domesticate the scuttle.
Triangular, behind, between the shoulders
Pinned neatly with one pin, with two before,
A many-colored, fringed silk-handkerchief,
And, crossed upon the breast, discovers bare
The neck in front, and spotless white shift hem,
And cross of gold and manifold gold chain.
Add to the older women gray hairs, wrinkles,
And rosaries, plump red cheeks to the younger,
Prayerbooks to all, white handkerchiefs in hand,
And in groups mix them, six or seven together,
Women and men, all seemly and decorous,
All going our way, all from church returning,
Under the blue sky, on the bright white road,
Up the right bank of the descending Drau,
Corn-harps on either hand and barberry bushes,
With here and there a tall larch intermixed,
A straggler from th' innumerable host
Encamped with outspread waving banners green
Upon the Helmberg's side, that on our left
To the sky rising slope shuts out the south,
And you 've the picture I 'd fain set before you.
Group after group drops off, each at its own
Familiar, well-trod turning, and we 're left
To follow on, alone, our upward way
To Untervierschach, where, beside the well,
With odoriferous horse-mint bordered round,
And yellow trollius and forget-me-not
And brightest eyebright, pansy and parnassia,
We sit a while upon the wooden bench
And drink the cool, clear water, and with sad
And unavailing pity hear the splash

Of the poor prisoners in the iron-clamped,
Padlocked vivarium, and, ashamed, reflect
On the atrocious uses to which man
Turns his superior intellectual power,
And domineers, the tyrant of creation.
On still, between the Drau upon our right,
And clay-slate Helmberg's thickly pine-clad side,
To where aloft upon its rugged knoll
The church of Upper Vierschach to the clouds
Points temerarious, tempting high heaven's wrath,
And over Helmberg's side low sunken now
Into an humble spur stand full in view,
Dark underneath the overhanging sun,
Innerfeldkofel's dolomitic mass
— Bitopped Tirol Parnassus, should the muse
Seek ever a Parnassus in Tiròl —
And the saw teeth of mightier Zwölfer-Kofel,
And the dark. fringing pine woods underneath.
Patches of snow in the ravines declare
Winter reigns there secure even in July.
In Innichen at one we lunch on soup
And bread and wine, and — delicacy here,
Thirty five hundred feet above the sea —
A pound of ripe, red cherries. Forth at two,
And Innichen's Black Bear behind us left,
And Landlord Tagger, and Saint Michael's church,
And good Saint Candid's bones in the Stiftskirche
— Payment in kind's fair payment, and saint's bones
No ill devised return for saint's belief,
And no one knew this better than pope Hadrian,
Nor many worse than Innichen's devout —
And, cast a parting look upon the site,
No more now than the site, of wealthy, old,
Roman Aguntum — see us toiling up
The grassy, green, irriguous watershed,
Which from the near Rienz and Adriatic,
Towards the far Danube, turns away, and Euxine,
The Drau's stream in the Rohrwaldberg just born,
And little of this wicked world's ways wotting.

Hid jealously as Nile's, the springs of Drau,
High on the mountain's side among the larch.
We see and hear the scanty, trickling stream,
As from the region of the clouds descending,
But leave the task to Trinker to climb up
Some ten years hence, and vaunt himself discoverer
Of the then first discovered springs of Drau.
And now we 've reached at last the tall, red cross,
Which on the watershed conspicuous
Looms to both valleys, and Rienz invites us
Down with him westward to episcopal
Brixen, and Brenner's foot, and deep broad Adige;
But we, by all his promises unallured,
Turn south the path up he has just come down,
Directest path to Italy and the vine.
Come with us, reader, lover of the vine,
Come with us, lover of unclouded skies,
And learn it 's not form but bright light which makes
Italy beautiful and shames the north,
Beautiful no less than the south in form,
But treated as a stepchild by the sun.
Up, up the valley southward, up Rienz's
Descending stream along the bright, white road,
Where 's by the dolomite precipices left
Scarce space sufficient for the Toblach tarn,
And fringing pinus pumilo and larch,
And the Rienz, and us, and bright, white road.
Not without tinge perceptible of green
The crystal of ferruginous Rienz,
Nor with brown rust unstained the dolomite
Pillows and bolsters of his oft-made bed.
Gray dolomitic peaks on either side
To the sky towering and, by hunter's foot
Or nimbler chamois, if ascended ever,
Ascended rarely, guard both road and river,
And on the traveller threatningly look down.
Welcome appears in view at half past six
The lonely inn of Landro, our night quarters,
Not for the first time now found hospitable,

And, rarer virtue, honest. Early supper,
Bed early, and sound sleep, and we awake
Alert next morning to pursue our journey.

Up the Rienz still in the gorge's bottom
Under the blue sky of July the sixth,
Our smooth road of white dazzling dolomite
Between the fringing larch invites us on,
Oft chiding our improvident delay,
Now to see cloudless, high Drei Zinnen Spitz,
Now to see blended Dürrensee's Rienz
With the Rienz of high Drei Zinnen Spitz.
Nor these our only loiterings, for behold,
Darkening our eastern sun, green Hohe Alm,
And in black shadow in the Dürren lake's
Transparent ripple riding, and see there,
Monte Piano and the rustic inn
Of Schluderbach, and to the east away,
The peaks Cadini, and we 've reached at last
The summit of the pass, and great Cristallo
Looks down upon us from our southern zenith,
As we stand reverent at the cross's foot,
Under the flaming brow of Croda Rossa[1],
Northward; but not stand long; some lemon thyme,
And blue phyteuma, gathered, and gnaphalium,
And dryas octopetala, and one blushing
Red rhododendron, and two yellow poppies,
We 're on our downward way toward Peutelstein,
Terror no longer now to the Tiròl,
Fortress no longer now of Adria's consort.
High on its isolated rock it stands,
The owl's nest and the adder's, in and out
The bat flits through its windows, and each time
The withering ivy polype looses hold,
A stone plumps heavy down into th' abysm.
We leave the road to swing in long zigzags
Backward and forward on the castle's right

---

[1] Germ. Hohe Gaisl.

Down to the Boite,[1] and ourselves the shorter
Precipitous path take on the castle's left
Through the pine wood, and 'cross the insecure,
Tottering foot-bridge, and with the tumbling torrent
Down the deep splintered, rocky, rough ravine,
Into the Boite valley, to the rock's
And castle's southward, where the Boite meets us
Side by side trending due south with the road,
And we have turned our backs on Peutelstein.
From time to time, as we descend the valley,
Our upturned eyes reverted seek its dark
Towering profile, against the blue sky, first,
Later against the background of the mountains.
And now we exchange — obliging so our patient
Laborious indefatigable feet
And dazzled eyes — the dusty, gravelly. new,
For the green moss-grown, old road, parallel.
Weighty the air with odours; here the rape,
There the delicious bean; and trollius sows
With golden globes the meadow, and spiraea
Blooms aromatic on the ditch's slope,
And stately heracleum to the full
Expands its rugged leaves and umbels white,
And cirsium eriophorum, not yet blown,
Brings to our minds back high Pregratten-thal,
Windisch Matrey, and Virgen, and the great,
Snowy Venediger's pretorian tent
Girt round with precipices, clouds, and gletschers;
And, on our guide's most uncomplaining shoulders,
Canny beside our wallets slung our cirsium
— Noli me tangere — eriophorum thyrse.
`At half past one Cortina di Omperzo
With no mean hospitality receives us,
Rests, but not long detains; nor turn we now,
As erst, our devious steps capricious westward
Into the mountains of Livinallongo,

---

[1] Sign. E. Jauer found the name written Boite in two geographical works,
but could not ascertain or even guess its gender. May, 1867.

In order to salute at Primiero
Our once good friend, il Giudice Negrelli.
Times have changed face since then, and with the times
What is't not changes? Whiter now my hair,
Stiffer my joints, my heart less warm and trusting,
And I love friends by just so much the less,
As three years changes have made clear to me
How much three years ago I over-rated
The stock to my account in friendship's bank:
And even were I less changed, mind and body,
And still at Primiero — not removed
To Mori — my good friend il Giudice,
And with these changing three years changed as little,
Still I 'd look twice now ere I 'd plunge, as then,
Into the mountains of Livinallongo
And Paneveggio and San Martin,
Without a road, without a guide, and scarce
With even a shed to shelter me a-nights
Against Jove Pluvius descending oft
In fire and thunder from the aerial Croda
Di Janis.

        So right southward on, ahead,
The Boite faithful, on the right below us,
Along the rugged base of Malcuore
High on our left, and through the Scotch-fir wood,
And past the roadside chapel on the right
Above the Boite's bank and Chiapuzza,
Where kindly from a shower nine months ago
The Virgin sheltered us returning northward
From old Bassano and our last year's journey;
And, crossed the Italian frontier,[1] reach at six
San Vito the first town, and sup and sleep
Under Malcuore, on the Boite's bank
Opposite the giant heights of Croda Pelmo.

Mountains have fallen a-nights and in their ruins
Buried whole villages, but none on us

---

[1] In the pine wood, two miles north of Chiapuzza (or qu; S. Vito).

Fell lást night, and we slept safe and undoubting
Even at thy foot, O treacherous Malcuore,
Who in one night o'erwhelmed'st in one grave
— It 's twenty years ago come Martinmas —
All Taulen's sleeping souls and Marceana's.
We sleep safe, and awake safe, and the graves
Of those tread thoughtful, who, asleep like us,
To a new day woke never. Left behind
At Borca the not too long to be trusted
Malcuore ridge, we come beneath the safer
Pyramidal shadow of Mont Antelao
Across the Boite flung and Boite valley
Like a black carpet. Other side the shadow
The post house of Venàs ere noon receives us
Remembered friends, and shelters from a shower,
And entertains with bread and wine and coffee.
Refreshed and rested, forth again at one,
And forward with the Boite, she below
Deep in her grassy, village-sprinkled holms,
We with the road high on the mountain's breast
In and out winding, inward winding most,
To cross, high up, the Vallesina torrent
Down through the left-hand clefts impetuous rushing —
Pray God it sweep not Vallesina with it,
Hamlet and mill and holm, into the Boite!
In Valle the road parts us at the fountain
In the piazza, and goes round by Jai,
Close under the Cadore painter's birthplace —
Fit birthplace for a painter, picturesque
Pieve di Cadore, in its nook
Amidst aerial woods and precipices.
We, with the Boite, take the shorter route
Direct down the ravine to Perarolo.
Our path 's the old road many a year disused,
Broken and rough, and furrowed deep by torrents
Blockaded here by landslips from above,
Or rock detached, or arms of trees, projecting;
There crumbling to the Boite far below,
Now turning to the right, now to the left,

Ascending now, and now again descending,
Tortuous as wounded snake; scarce foot-wide now
Edging the bare abysm and bed of Boite,
And now a yoke of oxen some ten yards
Might jolt a cart along what once was pavement.
At half past three we issue with the Boite,
At Perarolo, out of the ravine,
We to the coffee-house beyond the bridge,
The Boite underneath to the Piave.

And now along the right bank of the waters
Of the Piave and the Boite blended
Together in one vast, wide gravelly bed,
We follow on, at four, our southward way.
Above us on our right the mountain flank,
Under our feet the road we had left at Valle;
Below us on the left the united rivers
Wafting on rafts down to the Adriatic
The red pine of Friuli; opposite,
The left-hand mountain range shuts out the east,
And with the right-hand vies precipitous,
Massy and bare and high and multiform;
Worn into dark pine-bearing clefts the sides,
Or seamed with cataracts white, a savage scene,
Yet not without all touch of loveliness:
Here the first mulberry greets us, and the first
Rubicund blushing, everlasting pea,
And red valerian; not a rocky ledge
Nor interspace between the rocks but glows
Vivid with rhododendron;[1] now and then
The walnut spreads above us, now and then
The white robinia bloom perfume's the air,
And through its soft green foliage peers at times
The silvery chalice of the hazel nut,
And ivy for the absence of the vine
Makes to the eye amends; anthericum's

---

[1] Saw no Rhodod: until we had passed Omperzo; watched for it in vain
from Perarolo to Amperzo — 1868. —

Heaven-pointing star erects his brilliant disk,
And on her lank stalk columbine droop graceful.
Even in the wide, waste, gravelly river bed,
Patches of hemp refresh the eye not seldom,
Even on the rugged mountain's arid side
Not seldom hangs the grassy green plough furrow,
And the stream turns the mill wheel, and the saw
Up and down in the log plies, up and down,
And up and down, and up and down, incessant.
And now, behold, at Castel di Lavazzo,
Though still the scene be rude and rough the sky,
Great Bacchus' glorious gift, the vine, at last,
The graceful, fair, delicious, joyous vine!
If, Pentheus like, in my audacious youth,
I ever slighted thee, maligned thee ever,
Forgive my truly penitent gray hairs,
O thou nepenthe, sole not fabulous.
If there 's a cup in yonder Longarone,
It shall be drained to night to that God's honor,
Who speaks plain truth and quirks eschews and riddles.

> To Bacchus ever fair and ever young,
> Bacchus, the muse's friend, the friend of song,
> The thyrsus in his hand, the ivy crown
> About his brows from lofty Nysa down
> In chariot drawn by tigers, see, he comes
> A conqueror: twirl your timbrels, beat your drums.
> To civilize your savage western plains
> He brings the pampinus twisted in his reins.

Such was my palinode as from the hill
Of Castel di Lavazz' I followed down
The windings of the road to Longarone,
One short mile, where our worthy host Marina,
Shows to the curious traveller to this day,
The butt from which I libated to Bacchus.

To day an opener prospect spreads before us,
Over our heads expands a milder sky:
Not issued yet, we 're issuing from the mountains,
Not in the plains yet, we 're fast drawing nigh.

Passed on the right, two hours from Longarone,
The road by which last autumn we emerged
From old Bassano, Feltre, and Belluno
Into these Alpine heights, we reach ere noon
Capo di Ponte and Piave bridge,
Where the Piave, by a fallen-down mountain
Stopped in its southern course, wheels sudden west
To make its long detour round by Belluno,
And turns his back for aye on Serravalle.
Four hard boiled eggs, four cups of strong black coffee,
Bread, and a pint of wine, and half hour's rest,
And forward 'cross the covered wooden bridge
Which spans the river where it 's narrowest hemmed
Between the steep slate scaurs, and up the hill
By the old road; high noon above our heads
Under our feet the white dust, at our heels
Our shadows shrunk to pigmies following close
In search you 'd say, of shelter from the glare.
Slate strata horizontal from the hill,
Naked above, with vegetation clothed
On either side, of loveliest softest green:
Wild vine and clematis and fair robinia
And blood-stained cornel and laburnum's sister,
Cytisus nigricans, part black, part yellow,
And lonicera odoriferous,
Its own twig with its own twig intertwined,
And round about wound with convolvulus sepium,
Fasces without the axes and the fear.
Various the panorama from the summit:
Behind us the Piave, and our walk
Of yesterday from Perarolo downward;
Belluno on the right, white in the sun;
Below us, on the left, the new road winding;
Before us Santa Croce's turquois lake
Reflecting eastward the green, sloping flank -
Of Croda Liscia, rippling on the west
Up to our onward road across the bottom;
Fadalto's fallen-down transverse ridge shuts in
The lake and southern prospect; half way up,

Our road, ascending from the lake and bottom,
Traverses Santa Croce's pendent village.
And now thou hast seen the panorama round,
What need 'st thou travel the way with me, reader,
Down from the hill along the lake and bottom
And up Fatalto's steep opposing glacis?
Go, thou art free, let loose from school and master,
To romp in the play-gróund an hour or so,
And take thine idle fling and spin thy top;
Or, if it suit thy wayward humor better,
Count up how often in one page Childe Harold
Knocks out the brains of Common Sense and Priscian.
Good bye! at half past four we meet again
At Cima di Fadalto, there it 's yonder,
That crow's nest on the ridge's airy summit.
I never was a cynic, never shunned
Human society, from praise or blame
Never away turned without tingling ear:
Yet I can bear to be a while alone
Left by the whole world with my muse and daughter,
And in such solitude feel so sweet contentment
That I start at a foot-sound or a voice,
And hear of readers in natura rerum
Existent, with such mingled doubt and fear,
And curiosity, as a child first time
Reads in his primer of great grisly bears,
Caymans [1] and crocodiles and roaring lions.
So take it not for personal, gentle reader,
That, without thought of thee or our appointment,
I had posted down from Cima di Fadalto,
And was already on the Lago Morto's
Desolate edge, when thou cam'st running after,
Crying "Stop, stop, and wait for thy companion."
Death is unlovely, and as death unlovely
The Lago Morto, so called not unaptly,
A dim, unsightly, joyless, sluggish pool,
Stretched oblong in the bottom like a ditch,

---

[1] Crocodilus Palpebrosus. Imp. Dict.

Between the bare and rugged mountains trending
Parallel southward on our right and left,
As we descend from Cima di Fadalto
To take our way along the eastern brink.
Strewed with loose stones the mountains, with loose stones
The water's edge: our road descends into,
And traverses, a wilderness of stones,   -
Dreary as that grim pass down which all roads
Converging lead out of the cheerful sunlight,
Not to emerge again; but we emerge,
Rounding at last the left-hand mountain's spur,
And under shadow of the first sweet chestnuts
Entering, well pleased, Negrisola's happier basin,
Where at the foot of beech-clad Monte Pizzoc
The downy peach hangs ripening in the sun,
And the black fig swells, luscious. Every stream
Turns a filanda wheel, and peasant girls,
With black eyes and black hair and sallow cheeks
And long bare arms, shift sleeves and purple skirts,
Sing merrily in chorus while they sit
Unravelling in hot water, and entwining
Into the wondrous, golden yellow thread,
The fragile filaments of the cocoon.
Only too full of life the lake, one green
Luxuriant bower of willows, reeds and alders,
Rushes, and irides, and white nymphaeas,
And trembling aspen, and Herculèan poplar,
And many a sedge by fair Cyrene loved
And used for binding of her long, dank hair.
Maize fields receive us next and aspens planted
Each side the road symmetrical; and Meschio,
Carrying the lake's superabundant waters,
Keeps joyful company with us on the left,
Towards Serravalle, where arrived at seven,
We leave *sub dio*, Meschio and maize fields,
An aspen-planted road, and in Cattina's
Excellent Osteria alla Porta,
Against the now sometime impending storm
And gathering night, seek shelter, sup and sleep.

Come Muse! we 've been too humble, singing always
Of roads and roadside inn and entertainment,
And tree and flower and shrub and nature's face,
In spiritual as in unspiritual
Often, alas! unlovely: let 's explore
A loftier region, twang a louder string.
Crowned heads inspire me now, and my base-born
Inglorious heart glows with a generous warmth,
The while of kings and kingly deeds I sing,
And prouder of myself grow and my species.
Time was, this Serravalle, which so loud
The wheel of the silk-spinner echoes now
And paper-maker, echoed other sounds,
And not shopkeepers here their petty trades
Plied diligent, but king Matruco's mailed
And booted spearmen shouted, laughed, and revelled,
And contributions for their royal master
Exacted at the sword's point from the traveller
Through Serravalle's narrow, dark defile.
Yonder behold high on the mountain side
The ruins of the den so royal once
Where the lord lion couched, and whence the roar
Issued that shook the hills round, and the valleys.
Defender of the faith, too, was Matruco,
Stout as was ever England's own eighth Harry,
Sharp cauterizing to the bone as ever
Spain's second Philip or his Duke of Alva;
No Christian, to be sure, but not the less
On that account intolerant of all
Heterodoxy, every step aside
From the high turnpike road direct to heaven.
One day from 'cross the sea a palmer gray
With staff and cocklehat came wandering by,
And, tired, in Serravalle pass sat down,
To rest a while and munch his mouldy crust
Not even with water or green cresses kitchened.
Not long he had sat there when a lady veiled
Came all alone upon her ambling palfrey,
And had passed on, but, "Bless thee, gentle lady,

Christ and Christ's virgin mother," said the palmer,
"And pass me safe through dangerous Serravalle."
The lady stopped, she was Matruco's daughter,
Young, lovely, and in secret heart a Christian:
"Take this gold ring, O reverend, holy father;
'Twill pass thee safe through dangerous Serravalle."
The lady ambled on; the gold ring safe
Through Serravalle's barred gates passed the palmer,
But king Matruco's daughter — ah! she died
The martyr's death in yonder castle's dungeon.
And king Matruco, 'mongst men while he lived,
Lived praised and glorified, and when he died
Was crowned with amaranth by his thankful Gods,
And bid sit down among them, and for ever
In heaven reign, as on earth he had reigned despotic.
Well done, my Muse, not badly sung this one,
Great, glorious king; come, let's have at another.
A Christian this, a meek, pacific Christian,
Who had learned to love his neighbour and to turn
To him who struck him on one cheek, the other.
On heaven his thoughts were fixed, his eyes on heaven,
As Cromwell pious, but he kept like Cromwell,
His powder dry, and twice a week his blunted
Battle-ax sent to the armourer's to be sharpened.
What wonder? for his arm was never not
In exercise, death dealing round, and terror,
And long forgot by Serravalle's serfs
Matruco's praises in the praise of Richard,
Princely Gueccelli's great and glorious son,
Of Cam's most noble house, who twice laid waste
With fire and sword Friuli's fertile plains;
Conquered in Udine's hard fought, bloody battle,
And Sacile took by storm and Spilimberg,
Killing the males, and home to Serravalle
Dragging the women captive, Christian women,
By Christian men made captive, who had first
In cold blood slain their husbands, sons, and brothers.
Go, sceptic reader, and his virtues con
Where on his royal herse they shine inscribed

In Saint Giustina's church in Serravalle.
Himself there too in sculptured marble, see,
Supine extended; pages at his feet
Stand weeping, in its scabbard, not far off,
Rusts his discarded sword, alas! no more
To desolate, in Christ's name and the Virgin's,
The Christian hearth, and from the Alps extend
To distant Udine and the Adriatic
The domination of Cam's noble house.
Hast seen and heard enough? or carest to hear
Further, how death surprised the warrior young,
In fata viridis concessit post
Egregia facta multa, or to learn
That the disconsolate widow, who this weight
Of monumental marble on the heads
Imposed of those grim cuirassed halberdiers,
(For power, when dead and rotten, what support
Fitter than arms, its sole support when living?)
Herself was a king's daughter, and in honor
And pious memory of th' illustrious dead,
Regale monumentum hoc paravit
Anno millesimo trigesimo
Et quinto decimo salutis mundi.
Of kings enough, but scarce enough of saints,
At least from me, thou 'st heard, so gird thee up,
And, if thou 'rt well in wind, yon calvary
From station climb to station — nay, don't start;
I didn't say, on thy knees, but I'll not press thee,
For the hill 's steep and thou perhaps art tired,
Or not in the pat humor, yet it had led thee
Up to the very sanctum of the saint;
For dynasties are changed not here alone
In Serravalle, but in highest heaven,
Since king Matruco's daughter with her life
The forfeit paid of her apostacy,
And Saint Agosta 's worshipped in the cell
In which the renegade Agosta suffered.
So be it; old Father Time 's a harlequin
Has many a queer trick on his magic wand;

And who knows but he 'll yet with such a slap
Come down on thee and me as to transform
Me all at once into a master poet,
Thee, dreaded critic, into a disciple?

Between two rows on either side of green
Acer negundo, a delicious shade
Conducts us hence to Ceneda, a mile,
Though straight and flat, not tedious, nor at times
Not with gleditschia triacanthus varied,
And morus papyrifera and sumach,
All old friends, not before met on this journey.
Nor left behind with Ceneda the cool
Embowering shadow of the promenade,
And recognition glad at every step,
Of some well loved, and once familiar, face
Estranged by absence, but forgotten never:
Tall cypresses impervious to the light
Pillar with stately shafts, on either side,
The straight white road, with broad catalpa leaves
And oriental platanus overhung,
And the red clustering corals of ailanthus.
Beyond the promenade the road receives us,
Straight too, between deep ditches, in whose bottom
Ducklings swim joyful down the limpid stream.
Innocent souls, be happy while ye may
And not yet at your throats man's butcher knife
Ruthless, inexorable, bloody, cruel,
Humane, believe himself, and heaven-inspired.
Ay, to be sure! for what else is man's God,
Man's heaven, man's inspiration, but his own
Dira cupido? little ducks, swim on;
And chirrup, chirrup, on your native aspen,
Ye shrill cicadae orni; not so nice,
So delicately tutored is mine ear,
But it can bear your loud obstreperous song;
And on the bare bark lay thine eggs in peace,
And with fine russet sponge from evil eye,
And still more evil hand, securely cover,

Phlegmatic bombyx dispar, quaker dressed
All in one downy, velvet suit, cream-colored.
San Giacomo's park and ornamental gateways
And cheerful open village left behind,
And Colle on the hill passed on our left,
We follow on between sharp paliurus
And tall robinia hedges, our straight road;
Debouching with it, after three short miles,
Into the high post road from Pordenone;
And so, ere half past five, Conegliano
Reach tired, and entering by the boulevard
Le Fosse, take up quarters for the night
At the Campana, amid gardens glowing
Vivid with orange, lemon, and pomegranate,
Not without intermixture of our own
Hollyhocks stately, and red-blushing roses,
And aromatic pinks and gillyflowers,
And dahlias every colour on the prism.
Supper of rice minestra, ripe red cherries,
Cheese, wine, bread, apricots, and strong black coffee,
Rank poison to the sedentary, whether
Steady at home in easy elbow-chair,
Or jolting in malle-poste or railway carriage,
Or wheeling in a Báth-fly round and round
The pump-room after fugitive Hygeia —
Poison to all such bodies without legs
The hap-hazard medley, which, to us, provided
With Exercise's royal letters patent,
Is nectar and ambrosia and sweet health.
A half hour after supper at the window,
Snuffing the evening fragrance of the garden,
And marking how night's sentries one by one
Their stated posts take on heaven's battlements.
At last to bed scarce willing yet, though tired,
To close our eyes even for a few short hours
On this mixed world of ugliness and beauty
Sushine and shadow, pleasure, pain and death.

Friday, July the tenth, ere six o'clock

The bustle of the market underneath
Our bedroom windows, wakes us, as unwilling
To exchange a world of dreams for a real world,
As, some few short hours since we were unwilling
To exchange a real world for a world of dreams.
But, willing or unwilling, man must waken,
And, willing or unwilling, man must sleep,
And, willing or unwilling, man must dream;
Or it may hap must nót dream, as the moment,
His stern, uncompromising, arrogant,
Imperious, unrelenting, cruel mistress
In her caprice commands; so we awake,
And for th' adventures of another day,
If rightly called adventures, our day's petty
Vicissitudes of hot, cold, wet and dry,
Uphill and down hill, baiting, rest and motion,
Gird ourselves, up, alert, and forth, at eight,
By boulevard and promenade and road,
Under the clear blue sky and burning sun,
Or, as it may be, in the pleasant cool
Of overshadowing gleditschia standards —
Ah, that so fair a tree bore thorn so cursed! —
And broad catalpas and julibrasins,
And trembling aspens intertwined with vines,
Strangers as yet, and long may they be strangers.
To foul oidium taint; and guelder rose
Studs with its full white moons the maple hedge,
And stiff, old-maid stenactis borders, prim,
The broad ditch slope, and sallower beside
Tall saponaria's flaunting muslin white,
Droops sallow comfrey, and alisma bathes,
And watercresses, in the ditches bottom;
And far and wide spiraea over all
Flings lavish from her censer spiced perfume.

Why stands before the widower's troubled eye
His long lost loved one, at this moment why?
Plain as twelve years ago he saw her stand,
A ragusine centaurea in her hand,
Chance picked up relic of green house and home,

93

The sad day she set out strange lands to roam
With him and her one child, and now she 's gone;
And with his child the widower left alone
The useless sigh to heave, and tear let fall,
Upon a flower plucked from thy castle wall,
Sweet Susigana — see it 's the pale green [1]
Downy, gold-crowned centaurea ragusine.

Uncultivated either side the stream
A whole long mile the bed of the Piave,
Here met again returning from its round
By Feltre and Belluno, and bridged over
Gravel and stream four hundred metres wide;
A goodly work to see, and not less useful
Than to see goodly, specially to us
Whose dinner waits beyond at Spresiano.
So, paid the toll and crossed the bridge, and cleared
The waste offside of the Piave bed,
We reach ere noon and dine at, Spresiano,
On sliced polenta pudding and bean soup,
And fresh anchovies from the Adriatic,
Unused until to day to swim in wine.
Forward again at one, and from beneath
Warm glowing summer's lofty sapphire arch,
Look back on cloudy winter's cold white tents
Pitched far and wide upon the alpine summits.
And pleased compare our skill strategical
With Hannibal's: then right about and southward.
But not long we 're contented, discontent
Being the one thing indispensable
Not to man only but to all that lives.
For what is life but action, and to action
What other stimulus than discontent?
Sultry the air, the sun's rays hot and burning,
Dusty the road, we 've dined and we are thirsty.
Water 's the cry, but no where 's to be found,
Except in the frogs' puddle, even so much
As one drop; ah, were it only for a moment,

---

[1] The leaves and stalk are nearly white, resembling white cloth.

Give us the mountains back, and clear cool stream,
Even the snow and rain — but see! a shop
With bottles on a table at the door,
Box of cigars, a lemon and a tumbler.
We can yet punch here if we can't get water.
But we get water, for it 's a water shop,
And three centesimi pay for every glass,
Pure, or with lemon flavored, or rosolio,
Or milky with stomachic aniseed
Dextrously squirted out through the corked bottle's
Scrimp crow quill. Nor on us alone work potent
The plumb meridian rays; in all Madonna
Di Rovere village not one soul is stirring,
Not even a dog abroad, and jealously
— As if, within, Mars had again met Venus —
Closed in Di Tressa's villa every pane
Of the innumerable-paned casino,
Against the prying, penetrating God.
The stones our feet scorch, and, methinks, the air
Grows hotter with the chirp of the cicadae,
And counter-croak incessant of the frogs.
So, not unwelcome, opens at a quarter
Past four, Treviso's city gate before us,
And the cool shade of curtained porticoes
And awnings, and we hear the pleasant bubbling
Of fountains and the murmur of the Sile,
And in the molineto sup beside
The clattering mill-wheel and fast-rushing race;
Not ill pleased to enjoy until tomorrow
Rest and the shadow, or, if it likes us better,
In Giacomelli's garden, promenade
Among the dates and cactuses and yuccas;
Or wherebetween two fair Aralias shoots
Stately to heaven green stripling Araucaria,
Joyous, and of his south-sea home forgetful;
And old man Pilocereus far has wandered
From his companions, and our pity claims
For his decrepitude and long gray hairs;
Or onward where dianthoidean, blue

Tillandsia, feeds on air, and sago lurks
Nutritious in the cycas revoluta,
And coffee for the heart of man prepares
Her salutiferous enlivening beverage,
And bids him not to envy Jove his nectar;
And erudite papyrus his days passes
In well earned golden leisure: or at last
Tired sauntering, sit down in the tent pitched for us
By pendulous Japonic sophora,
And look up at the hara bicolor
To and fro swinging in his airy cage
Armillary, and in our hearts almost
Quarrel with Nature who such gorgeous plumage
Married capricious to that odious voice.
Home to the molinetto then, and bed,
And dreams of our long journey almost finished,
And sandy deserts and siroccos sultry,
And thirst and parched lips, and a sound confused
Of clattering mill-wheels and fast-rushing water,
And whispering arbours cool and crowing cocks,
And Guinea-fowl in cages, crying go-ak.

    Next morning early a new sun awakes us,
With as bright golden light from face and shoulders,
And every chrysolite and carbuncle
And stud phosphoric of his chariot, streaming,
And every sparkling diamond of his harness,
And bids us welcome to Osiris' city,
Worthy at least one whole day to detain us
Well worthy, were it only for his sake
Who, born within its walls, slept not content
Till in Rome's walls he had made him such a breach,
That he could in and out and back and forward
Pass when he liked with all his Gothic host,
No leave of gate asked or of pope or caesar.
In vain we search; in all Treviso no one
Of Totila knows more than that he saw
The light first somewhere in, or near, Treviso:
What wonder? we have as vainly sought in Andes

And Padua for the cradles of their heroes.
Ah Time, that wouldst be called an honest landlord,
Yet in thy care to let thy lodgings clean
And unincumbered, sweep 'st out not alone
The dust and rubbish of th' outgoing tenant,
But, with th' exception of some massy piece
That *mole sua* firm stands and defies thee,
Even the very furniture and goods
He has left behind to thy safe care and keeping.
Ah Time, not even thrifty, where are now,
The relics of the eleventh Pope Benedict,
Treviso's Bocasini wise and good?
Strange to Treviso's ears the very name;
We said or thought as up the stair we turned
Into the Mont di Pieta to see
The body of the Saviour borne by angels,
One of the massy pieces left behind
By George of Castelfranco, and not yet
With all his will thereto cleared out by Time.
I never was a connoisseur in painting,
And least of all, not being myself religious,
In the religious genre: angels' wings
I have never yet seen, don't so much as know
Where the angel wears his wings, on his travelling cap,
And travelling staff and boots, like Maia's son,
And so must go to seek them when he wants them;
Or, peacock-fashion, handy on his back,
And needing only to be fairly spréad out.
So of Georgione's angels I'll say nothing,
And, with respect to his dead Christ, but hint
I had liked it better had the legs been matches.

    Spacious the old cathedral of Treviso,
Saint Peter's, founded by Prosdocimus
In honor of his teacher, anno fifty —
Pity no stone remains of the first walls!
We stay not long, for rococo the tombs
And thick with dust; the pictures black and mouldy;
Perspective architectural none, no shrines,
No stained-glass rainbows fascinate the eye

And almost lead the understanding captive.
The solemn waste but presses on the heart,
And drives out to the open air again,
And bright blue sky and sun and living world.

Sunday, July the twelfth, at half past nine
We bid our last farewell to old Tarvisium,
And through the Altinia portal hold our way
Along the level aspen-planted road
Dusty and white and straight, and Zaara hot,
Between its grassy, broad luxuriant ditches,
Deep in whose bottom butomus rears high
His purple standard over the clear water,
And vallisneria's brave Leanders swim
Ardent in search of their expectant Heros,
Nothing afraid, though all around them bristle
Sagittaefolia Sagittaria's arrows.
Lonely the road and still, as though remote
A whole week's journey yet the capital city.
Our footsteps' sound disturbs the frogs that squat
On the broad floating nuphar lutea's leaves,
Or shelter from the sun's rays in the typha,
And one by one, as we approach, they go
Plop plop into the water; azure bright
Sylphide libellulas flit silent-winged
From carex spike to carex spike; or poise
Weightless upon the filagree thalictrum;
And, timid, helpless, shy, and fugitive.
As harmless, the green lizard wares our coming,
And darts for safety to the nearest hole;
And, at long intervals, a basking adder
Starts, and away shoots rustling through the grass,
Not to be followed even if we were willing,
Even if we shared man's appetite to kill.
Dinner at half past twelve in Mogliano,
Where, from the flames resurgent, the Fenice
Friendly invites us in, and treats us to
Plentiful rice minestra and red wine,
And the acquaintance, for the nonce, of shipwrigut

Fracchia of Venice, here with wife and child
The days canicular villeggiaturing,
And leaving to his prentices to cobble
The battered British bark that has cleared out
In the warm sunny port of the lagoons,
And bounes it joyful for its well loved home
Of cloud and fog and smoke and liberty.
Ah Venice, Venice, thou whose gonfalon
Waved once from Cyprus to the banks of Garda,
Thou who thy royal nuptials solemnizedst
Yearly with Adria on Bucentaur poop —
Down on thy craven knees, and kiss the hand
That, raised to punish, graciously relents,
Takes off the interdiction, and restores thee
The Austrian free port's privilege and rank.
Thou mayst with industry and prudence yet
Grow rich again; and power with riches comes,
And power 's not far removed from domination.
Is it the Lion of Saint Mark I hear
Through his sleep growling, and the Lombard Biscia
Out of his covert answering with a kiss?
And is it only shadows of the clouds
Flitting across Verona's Alps I see
Northward, or trains of cannon, horse and foot,
In headlong route for Austria, *sauve qui peut?*

    Mestre at four, wide streeted, dull and lifeless,
Except some promenaders from the city,
If promenaders justly may be called
Who can't the city leave except by rail,
Or boat, and never but by omnibus
From railway station or the water's edge
Arrive in Mestre. Too late for the train,
And neither so brave nor so inexperienced
As to do battle with the barcajuoli,
We put up for the night in the Vapore,
Sup on fried liver and cappucci soup,
And drink our fraccolo, and go to bed,
And sleep as best we may, plagued all night long
By the zanzaras — sweet foretaste of Venice! —

Till the sun rising sends them tired, to sleep,
And full of blood, and, to supply their places,
Wakens fresh myriads of black buzzing flies.

Monday, July thirteenth, concludes our journey
By early train to Venice and our lodgings,
Once Petrarch's on the Ripa dei Schiaveni,
Opposite San Giorgio and the midday sun,
And 'cross the quay scarce thirty paces distant
From the up-splashing Adriatic wave,
First house beyond the Ponte del Sepolcro.
Islands, with churches crowned, bay-in the sea,
And streak with tower and minaret the horizon.
Long, narrow, noiseless, black as death or night,
Not rowed, but pushed by standing sculler onward,
Incessant gondolas glide to and fro,
Back, forward, left and right, in all directions;
Gay, if in silence can be gaiety.
With comers, goers, idle or on business,
Motley below our windows swarms the quay;
And gondoliers for fares call, and colporteurs
Offer for sale their wares, and watermen
Pump into barrels water from the main land,
In boats brought over to supply the wells
Of Venice, dried up by the July heat.
Our landlord Spindione Vianello,
Enriched by the monopoly, has honor
In Venice, as in Rome, once, Pluvius Jove.
      And now we 're safe in Venice, where art thou,
Reader? — in London, or New York, or Paris,
Or what yet greater city to be built
At the Nile's source, or by La Plata's wave?
What matter? . . thou and we are to meet never
Nearer than we have this day met each other,
Or any day, in thought, of this long travel.
Farewell, and whatsoever separate way
Thou strikest tomorrow, nothing fare the worse
That thou 'st so far with us in spirit travelled.
Nothing the worse fare, but the better rather;

And sometimes think with pleasure of thy friends,
The wandering Irish Gleeman [1] and his daughter,
No other pay they ask, no other beigh. [2]

---

[1] The Gleeman, the author of "The song of the Traveller," see Conybeare.

"The song of the Traveller professes to record the wanderings of a certain 'Gleeman' the contemporary of Eormanric and of Aetla. 375 — 433." — Guest. History of English Rhythms, vol. II. P. 76.

"The Gleeman was born among the Myrgings, a Gothic race dwelling on the Marches which separated the Engle from the Sweve, during the fourth and fifth centuries." Guest. Ibid. vol. II P. 397.

[2] Armlet — see "The song of the Traveller."

THE END.

www.ingramcontent.com/pod-product-compliance
Lightning Source LLC
Chambersburg PA
CBHW032151010726
47493CB00008BA/2662